Fern Verdant
& the Silver Rose

Fern Verdant
& the Silver Rose

Diana Leszczynski

Alfred A. Knopf   New York

Thanks to Bradley, Jane, Debra, Dalisa, Blaire, and especially Arlo Gordon and Claire Dinhut.

THIS IS A BORZOI BOOK PUBLISHED BY ALFRED A. KNOPF

Visit us on the Web! www.randomhouse.com/kids

Educators and librarians, for a variety of teaching tools, visit us at www.randomhouse.com/teachers

Library of Congress Cataloging-in-Publication Data
Leszczynski, Diana.
Fern Verdant and the Silver Rose / Diana Leszczynski. — 1st ed.
    p.   cm.
Summary: Fern Verdant's mother, a famous botanist, disappears just before Fern's thirteenth birthday, and when Fern discovers that she has inherited the ability to communicate with plants, she realizes that this is the only way she will be able to find and save her mother.
ISBN 978-0-375-85213-8 (trade) — ISBN 978-0-375-95213-5 (lib. bdg.)
[1. Human-plant relationships—Fiction. 2. Plants—Fiction.
3. Mothers and daughters—Fiction. 4. Kidnapping—Fiction.] I. Title.
PZ7.L5658Fe 2008
[Fic]—dc22
2008003545

The text of this book is set in 11.5-point Goudy.

Printed in the United States of America
November 2008
10 9 8 7 6 5 4 3 2 1

First Edition

For Pam Turk

Fern Verdant

"Why couldn't you have just given me a *normal* name?" Fern Verdant had asked her mother ever since she was very small. "You have no idea what it's like being a modern child!"

"*Normal?* What exactly do you think *normal* is?" Fern's mother, Lily, would ask, and then she would answer her own question. "*Normal* is a myth perpetrated by people afraid of the unique." Fern's father, Olivier Verdant, would nod in agreement.

"That's a very nice philosophy," said Fern, "but you try living my life."

Olivier Verdant was a French botanist who specialized in ferns. He adored ferns. He was a frequent contributor to the *American Fern Journal,* and spent his days conducting fern research in a massive greenhouse in the Verdants' backyard. It was his idea to name Fern, Fern. Every night as the Verdants ate dinner in their greenhouse, the ferns swayed and drooped around them, reminding Fern of her awful burden.

Fern's mother was also a botanist, as if one in the family wasn't enough! At first Fern was happy that ferns weren't her mother's specialty, but as she grew older she wished they were. Lily Verdant traipsed around the globe saving endangered plants. If there was a last languishing lotus flower in Udaipur or a fatally failing tea tree in Australia—Lily was there to save it. Once she had gone all the way to Peru to revive the sole survivor of an exotic strain of poppy. At least Fern knew she could always find her father huddled in the greenhouse studying his ferns, while her mother could be off anywhere in the whole world. Fern suspected that her parents might be guilty of neglect.

Lily and Olivier were very happy together. They'd met when Olivier was an exchange student from Paris, France. It was true love, spurred by a mutual and feverish fascination for botany. They botanied their way through college and they botanied their way into marriage. Fern was their only child. She hated plants as much as her parents loved them. It was because of botany that the family now lived in the miserable town of Nedlaw, Oregon.

The Verdants had once lived in a different town where Fern had had a best friend. It was the home of a university with the most important botany school in the world. Students from around the globe came to study there. The Verdants had many friends among the faculty, and the many friends each had one child because they were all far too busy researching to have more. Fern's best friend was Ivy Friedrichs. Ivy's father was also a botanist. Fern and Ivy both wished their parents were something more normal than botanists, like doctors or lawyers.

One day, while poring over specimens, Olivier Verdant discovered a brand-new fern. Its natural habitat was in the Pacific Northwest near the town of Nedlaw.

"I think we should move there so you can properly study your fern," suggested Lily, who was very supportive of Olivier's career. Fern was miserable. Not only did she have to say goodbye to Ivy, she now had to compete for her parents' affection with the Verdant Fern. It was like having an evil twin.

"One day you'll understand," Lily said to her daughter. "You'll love plants just as much as we do." Fern couldn't believe how little her mother knew her.

The day they moved to Nedlaw was the saddest day of Fern's life. Ivy and Fern clung to each other and cried their eyes out. Their parents placed comforting arms on their daughters' quivering shoulders, but exchanged knowing glances that said "They'll get over it soon." The Verdants arrived in Nedlaw, home of the Verdant Fern, and the bleakest, grayest, most horrible place Fern had ever seen.

Nedlaw had a quaint, old, recently renovated main street with three Starbuckses. It was surrounded by sprawling subdivisions with snaking arms that reached out like the asphalt veins in a witch's hand. Beyond the town, thick forests made their way down to sheer cliffs that dropped off into the black ocean. Fern wondered what the point of being near an ocean was if you couldn't even swim in it because the weather was so cold and wet all the time.

"All the better for ferns," said Olivier, smiling happily. Outside of town, near the forest, the Verdants bought a hundred-year-old red-brick farmhouse. Behind it they built the greenhouse.

Fern was enrolled at Joan Baez Middle School. When Nedlaw was just a village, the singer had passed through, and loved the town so much that she performed a concert to raise money for the local school. The townsfolk renamed the school in her honor. Most of the kids at Baez were the children of commuters. Every morning hundreds of fathers in crisp suits took the train to the city. Fern wished her own father would take a train somewhere like all the others. They had real jobs. Instead, Olivier walked around in dirty boots, wearing a thoughtful expression. Fern couldn't understand how studying a plant was a proper job.

When Lily wasn't off rescuing disappearing dahlias or vanishing violets, she drove Fern to school. Lily was beautiful, but she dressed with no regard for fashion. She wore shoes with heels that went down instead of up, and clothes that were baggy and bland. Lily had to know exactly how each person who made her clothes was treated at their place of work. How much were they paid? Were the working conditions safe and sanitary? Lily needed to know that they were treated fairly in order to buy their goods. Shopping with Lily was excruciatingly embarrassing for Fern.

Many of the other mothers in Nedlaw also worked, but when they dropped their daughters off at school they wore tall stiletto heels that made them look like lanky blue-suited

4

gazelles. Their hair was straight and shiny, as was their daughters'. They all looked perfect. Lily's hair looked like birds were nesting in it. She barely ever cut it, and jet-black curls shot out of her head like startled slinky toys. Her skin was tawny from being outdoors. Her eyes were piercing blue. She definitely stood out in a crowd. Fern looked exactly like Lily; they were two peas in a pod.

Being the new kid at school is bad, but being the new kid in baggy organic cotton clothing made by well-paid Peruvian seamstresses with full health benefits and child care, and being dropped curbside by Lily Verdant's beat-up blue Volvo station wagon, was miserable. The kids at Joan Baez Middle School looked at Fern like she was a freak. These same kids would all graduate into high school together. Fern figured she'd be in college before she ever had a friend again.

One day, shortly after they'd arrived in Nedlaw, Lily received a telephone call from a man named Claude Hubris. He told her he had a desperately ill rose. Among Claude's prized cultivations were roses as blue as the sky, as green as limes, as black as the night, and so yellow that like the sun it hurt if you looked at them. Hubris roses were world-renowned; some sold for thousands of dollars. Once Claude had sold a rose to an Indian prince for a million rupees, which is a lot of money, but not nearly as much as you'd think. The ailing rose was a Silver Rose, the only one of its kind in the world. Claude told Lily the Silver Rose was on its last petals, and begged her to come and heal it.

Lily picked up Fern from school, and told her she was leaving town the next day on some botany business. That evening

5

they prepared a special farewell dinner together. It was raining outside, but the kitchen was warm. A symphony of lids rattled on simmering pots and pans. Moisture drizzled down the windows, fogging out the rest of the world. Cooking with Lily was always a challenge because she only ate fruits, nuts, and certain vegetables. It amazed Fern that Lily could make such delicious dishes from so little.

They ate dinner in the greenhouse. When they had finished, Lily asked Fern to take the dirty dishes into the kitchen. She leaned over and whispered to Olivier, "I feel badly about having to leave again. Fern's not very happy here in Nedlaw, and she hasn't made many friends yet, but I have to go."

"She'll be fine," Olivier tried to comfort his wife. "*We'll* be fine." He put his arm around her.

After dinner Fern and Lily went for a walk down to the steep cliffs that loomed along the coastline. They listened to the waves crash against the rocks and looked out over the never-ending nothingness of the sea.

"Just imagine," Lily said, smiling, "across that ocean Chinese people are having tomorrow, yaks are climbing Tibetan mountain peaks, Arabian horses are galloping across sandy dunes . . . and a beautiful teal tulip is blooming in a Tunisian garden. Isn't it wonderful?" But all Fern saw were dark, bleak waves.

"It looks like the end of the world to me." Fern was quiet for a moment, then she said something that had been on her mind for a long time. "I don't understand why you and Dad bothered to have a kid when you love plants so much better."

Lily looked at Fern, startled. She drew her daughter close to her. "That's not true. I love you so much it hurts my heart sometimes. I love plants in an entirely different way. Just wait, one day you will, too, and it will be something special we can share."

Later that night, as Fern was about to fall asleep, Lily came into her room with a flowerpot. In the flowerpot was dark, rich soil and a seed.

"I brought you a present. It's a very special seed. You must care for it and keep it near." All Fern saw was a stupid pot of soil.

"Don't worry, I won't be gone long." Lily kissed her daughter on the forehead and switched off the light. Fern got out of bed and looked at the "present" on her bedside table. She was furious. What kind of mother could think that a pot of dirt would make her feel better? Most mothers would get their daughter a dress, something pretty, not a pot of dirt. To Fern this was further proof that her mother didn't care for her at all.

"I really do have unfit parents," cried Fern. She opened her bedroom window and angrily threw the flowerpot outside. The pot hit a large weeping willow, gashing the tree. The broken shards scattered on the ground. Fern fell onto her bed and cried.

The next morning she sulked her way downstairs to breakfast. Olivier made some marvelous French toast with blackberries, and they all ate in the greenhouse. Fern only picked at her food. Lily's suitcase was brought downstairs and loaded into the trunk of the car. It was gray and misty outside, as usual. They all drove to the train station together. Fern barely spoke the whole way there. She stared sullenly out the window. At the station

Lily hugged Fern tightly, but Fern refused to hug Lily back. Lily kissed her husband goodbye and boarded the train. She stuck her head out the compartment window as the train pulled out of the Nedlaw station. The mist clung to her curls and glistened. Lily waved and Olivier waved back. Fern stared angrily down at her feet.

Neither Olivier nor Fern could have guessed that Lily would not return to them.

Lily's Nightmare

When Lily Verdant's train pulled into a small station near the house of the Hubrises, a purple car that looked like a speeding bruise screeched into the parking lot. The driver stepped out to greet Lily. He had a shock of bright green hair, like fuzzy lichen. Lily was not prejudiced against anyone with colored hair. In fact, a very good friend of Lily's from college had dyed her hair red and blue and orange, and Lily loved it. This green hair was not dyed. It was real. The driver looked like a giant Chia Pet or a Chia Man.

Lily tried not to be rude, but it was hard not to stare. She said she'd prefer to walk, but the Chia Man said it was too far. He hustled her into the car, and then tore down the dark dirt road toward the Hubris home. Lily looked anxiously out the windows at the forbidding landscape. Sharp cliffs protruded over a frantic sea. If the Silver Rose hadn't been in trouble, Lily wouldn't have been caught dead in this place.

Claude and Luella Hubris greeted Lily at the door of their enormous Victorian home. The house heaved in the gusting wind, like it was trying to spit something out. Claude was so deeply tanned it was distracting. The tan made his teeth look wickedly white. He wore a white linen suit and a Panama hat, like he'd woken up on a Caribbean island but had somehow ended up here. His fingernails were manicured and shiny. He smiled and shook Lily's hand.

Luella was strange. Her alabaster skin looked as though it had never seen the sun. A smile like a fat red lightning bolt was smeared across the bottom of her face. Her eyes screeched back toward her ears, as though they were fleeing her nose. Around her bony shoulders she wore a finely woven fuzzy black shawl made from live caterpillars, their little heads hanging down like a forlorn fringe. A knee-length red leather skirt hugged Luella's narrow hips, revealing green stockings woven from spiderwebs. She teetered on a pair of blue snakeskin stilettos. There wasn't a thing on her that hadn't once been, or wasn't still, alive, including the two monarch butterfly barrettes that held her thick blond hair in place. The butterflies flapped their wings, their wide eyes begging for freedom. Her entire appearance was very disturbing. If it hadn't been for the rose, Lily would have fled.

Lily asked to see the flower immediately, but the Hubrises insisted on chatting. They gave her tea, which she did not drink, and inquired in great detail about her work. They poked and prodded and probed, but Lily ignored their questions and insisted she be taken to the Rose. She felt as though she were being interrogated. Finally, the Hubrises led her down a long hallway to a massive domed greenhouse. The Silver Rose was the only plant in the whole greenhouse. It sat forlornly on a marble pedestal.

Lily had never, ever seen anything like it. The Rose appeared to be made of real silver. Its petals were a metallic gray that looked like mother-of-pearl, only badly tarnished. The Rose drooped sadly. Lily opened up her black plant-doctor's bag and removed her equipment. She took the flower's temperature and examined its leaves. She checked the air, the soil, and anything else that could possibly be affecting the Rose's general health. The Hubrises watched. As Lily performed a thorough examination of her patient, she heard a whisper: "Please . . . I beg you . . . let me die." Lily gasped.

"What? What?" probed the Hubrises.

They had not heard the Rose. In fact, no one could hear the Rose, no one except for Lily Verdant, who was appalled by its wretched condition.

"It's not well at all." Lily was angry. "This rose is a victim of terrible abuse." Luella put her hand on Claude's sleeve. Lily could have sworn she saw the two of them exchange a sly smile.

"But who would do such a thing?" Luella asked, barely hiding her smirk.

"Can you save it? Please? We do love it so much!" Claude pleaded. Lily did not believe a word they said. She wanted to escape as soon as possible, but her conscience wouldn't let her.

She knew it would take time to heal the Rose, and she wasn't about to abandon a flower in need. The Hubrises asked her to stay in their mansion, but Lily had booked a room down the road at the Desolation Motel.

"Don't give up, please," Lily said to the Rose.

For the next three days Lily faithfully went to the Hubris mansion and tended to the flower. The damage was deep. The Silver Rose shuddered with fear every time the door opened. Lily was puzzled. How had the Hubrises created such a flower? It was definitely not a product of nature. Had they put mercury or silver dust in the soil? Whatever they'd done, they'd produced a beautiful but bleak plant.

On the third day Luella walked into the greenhouse. The Rose shrank slightly, sensing her putrid presence. Luella smiled, complimenting Lily on her work. The Rose looked healthier; its petals glowed.

"Have you any idea what this Silver Rose might fetch on the rare rose market? *This* could be a million dollar rose!" Luella bragged.

No, Lily thought to herself, *it will not be!* For Lily had decided then and there that she would return to the greenhouse under the cover of darkness and save the Rose that very night. She would turn it over to the Society for the Prevention of Cruelty to Plants, where it would be protected.

Later that afternoon, as Lily was about to leave the house of Hubris, she ran right into Claude, who stood blocking her exit.

"Hello, Mrs. Verdant. Our Rose is certainly looking better.

You obviously have an aptitude with plants . . . an extremely green thumb." Claude smiled an oily smile. "How much longer will it be until the Rose is back up to snuff?"

"Another day should do it," Lily responded, trying to inch past him.

"Won't you join us for supper . . . this once?" He smiled, the glare of his teeth temporarily blinding Lily.

"You're both horribly . . . kind, but I have work to do back at the motel."

"We insist," he added, sidestepping right in front of her.

"Then I'd like to freshen up." Lily turned on her heels and fled into the bathroom. Splashing cold water on her face, she realized it was now or never. She had to escape right away. Plucking a face towel from a pile on the black marble counter, she noticed a monogram in Gothic scroll. The letters *"HS"* were boldly embroidered.

HS? HS? she thought to herself. A loud banging on the door interrupted her thoughts. Lily stepped out, as cool as a cucumber. Claude clutched her shoulder with his tanned, manicured hand. His fingers dug into her as he steered her into a great dining room. Thunder rumbled outside. Rain pelted on the roof. Lily wriggled free of his grip. An icy chill flowed through her body. She pulled on her hemp jacket to stave off the cold. Luella arrived for dinner in a floor-length black leather gown. A live rabbit stole hung around her neck. The rabbits had been dyed yellow, and they were draped over her shoulders with a look of gloomy resignation. Lily was appalled.

"Sit!" Luella pushed Lily down into a chair.

"It's time we had a little talk," said Claude. "We have been informed that you appear to be quite special, that you have a remarkable gift. Somehow, if there's a dying dahlia in Columbia, or a perishing periwinkle in Madagascar, you seem to know about it before anyone else. How is that, Mrs. Verdant? What sort of special powers do you possess? And even more important, where do they come from?" All the color drained from Lily's face.

"Special?" Lily spoke in an uncertain voice. "Gift? I have no idea what you're talking about."

"Now, now," Claude said. "Let's not play games. We have a little proposal for you."

Chia Man brought out platters of roasted suckling pig and grilled trout.

"I'm a vegetarian." Lily hurriedly pushed her chair away from the table.

"Of course you are," snapped Luella.

"I'm really not hungry." Lily got up. Claude was about to push her back into her seat when she cried out.

"Wait! Did you hear that?"

The Hubrises hadn't heard a thing.

"Hear what?" said Luella.

"That noise!" Lily whispered. "Coming from the greenhouse."

"I didn't hear a noise." Claude was getting annoyed.

"There's something wrong with the Silver Rose." Lily pushed Chia Man out of the way. "It's in grave danger." Lily knocked her chair to the ground, blocking Claude. She ran toward the greenhouse. Claude and the Chia Man followed her down the hall. Luella trailed behind. Her dress was very tight and prevented anything other than the tiniest of steps.

Lily raced into the greenhouse, bolting the door behind her. She plucked the pot off its pedestal and hugged the Rose to her chest. Outside she heard a crack of thunder. Claude banged on the door.

"Open this door, you botanical twit!" he shrieked.

Rain pounded on the roof. Lily kicked at the glass panels of the greenhouse with all of her strength, but the glass was thick and wouldn't break. She kicked and kicked until finally her shoe shattered the glass. Lily and the Rose fled through the opening into the wet night. By the time Chia Man had pried the door open, Lily was disappearing into the dark.

Chia Man and Claude gave chase. The wind howled; the rain poured. It was quite difficult to make out a woman and a rose fleeing into the bleak night. Chia Man's bright green hair glowed in the dark. Lily ran as fast as her legs would carry her. In the gloom and the rain it was impossible for her to see more than three feet in front of her, so it came as a great surprise when the earth suddenly disappeared and she found herself hurtling over a cliff, plummeting through the dampness toward a wet, sandy beach far below.

Claude ran toward the cliff. He saw Lily vanish over the edge. Suddenly the rain stopped, and gray clouds parted to reveal a blue-black sky. The moon shone and revealed the beach below. Lily lay sprawled on her back in the sand, her pale face framed by a halo of inky curls. Claude saw the glint of the Silver Rose in the moonlight as it lay on Lily's chest.

"Oh, dear!" said Claude Hubris, gazing down at the unconscious woman. For a moment his face lost its color. Luella inched up behind him. She looked over the cliff and saw Lily Verdant lying as still as a stone. Her mouth fell open.

"Oh, no!" Luella's voice wavered. "We're in for it now!"

Grief

Fern and Olivier tried to piece together what had happened. Each day that Lily was away, she'd called home at least three times to check in with her family. Fern listened in on one call after Olivier thought she'd hung up. Lily told Olivier that she suspected some strange goings-on in the house of Hubris, but said she'd fill him in when she came home.

Fern had a creepy feeling. She went outside to the weeping willow tree and searched for the tiny seed her mother had given her. Once she found it, Fern replanted it in a new pot and placed it by her bedside. The next morning Olivier waited for Lily's call, but it never came. When he called the Hubrises, they said Lily had gone home. Olivier knew she'd done no such thing. He called the authorities and reported Lily missing.

Claude and Luella Hubris seemed shocked that Lily had

disappeared and told the police they'd assumed she was safe at home. They showed the authorities the fine work Lily had done with the Silver Rose. Upon examination, the flower appeared healthy. The Hubrises stated that it had been Lily's habit to walk along the cliffs between their home and the Desolation Motel. Perhaps the police should look there. Further investigation turned up a single Earth shoe and Lily's Peruvian hemp jacket.

Olivier and Fern went to see the Hubrises to investigate for themselves. Fern didn't like the look of Claude and Luella one bit. They seemed fake and sinister. The Verdants combed the coastline between the Desolation Motel and the Hubris mansion. Olivier retrieved Lily's possessions from her room. He rented a boat. Father and daughter went out onto the ocean, looking for they didn't know what.

"Maybe she's gone to China or Tunisia," said Fern.

"Your mother would never leave without telling us," answered Olivier. "Her love for us is deeper than . . ." He paused, unable to think of anything else that deep. They both looked out at the endless horizon thinking sad thoughts.

Back home Olivier wrote letters and e-mails to every botanist he knew. Had anyone seen Lily Verdant, darling wife, dearest mother, a botanist above botanists? But no one had. Olivier was so depressed that he was barely able to put his clothes on in the mornings. He lay in his bed staring at the ceiling. No words in the world could describe how Fern felt. She could not stop remembering how she had refused to hug her mother on the Nedlaw train station platform.

Olivier's mother, Grandmamma Lisette, flew in from France as soon as she heard that her daughter-in-law was missing. She made her son and granddaughter get out of their beds, and fed them tart tatin, croissants, and bowls of hot chocolate. She convinced them to get dressed and go out for some fresh air. Months dragged by. There was no news of Lily. Nothing. Summer arrived and the sun shone, but Fern and Olivier wanted no part of it. They preferred the gray gloom of their home, and kept all the curtains drawn.

Eventually Grandmamma insisted Fern must return to school. Sticking out like a sore thumb because of Lily was one thing, sticking out like a sore thumb because there was no Lily was another. Whispers skittered through the hallways of Joan Baez Middle School. Lily Verdant had disappeared or run away . . . or committed suicide. The mystery of Lily Verdant grew and grew. It followed Fern everywhere—in the cafeteria, and up and down Main Street. When people spoke with her, she could see the mixture of pity and curiosity in their eyes.

Two weeks before Fern's thirteenth birthday, Grandmamma noticed her granddaughter had sprouted up inches overnight. The clothes that had once hung on her loosely were now too small. Grandmamma noticed that her son was bent, curling up like a fern. Her family was gray and miserable. Nothing was helping.

"That's it!" Grandmamma announced to them. "You both need a change of scenery, something to help you get better. I insist that you come home with me." Two days later they were all en route to Paris, France.

The Vision

When they all arrived in Paris, Grandmamma hustled them into her ancient pink Mini Minor (a car the size of a large brioche), and drove them at ninety miles an hour through narrow streets to her apartment. Fern had not been to France since she was little and barely remembered a thing about it. It was so different from home. The air smelled delicious, and everyone dressed nicely.

Grandmamma Lisette immediately sent Olivier to the Jardins des Plantes (the Paris Botanical Gardens). Hundreds of years ago the gardens were planted with flowers and herbs so doctors could study how they cured the sick. Every day Olivier went to the gardens, lay in the grass, and breathed deeply. Tiny yellow chamomile buds released soporific pollen. Olivier finally slept, a clearheaded, deep, untroubled sleep. Grandmamma

Lisette knew that sleep would do Olivier a world of good. Each day he got a bit better and stood a little straighter.

Grandmamma Lisette wasn't sure what would help Fern. "You must feel what you feel," she said, "but don't let it drown you."

"I have a terrible secret, Grandmamma." Fern's head hung low. "The night before she went away, I was mad at my mom. I was mad because she was always away rescuing rotting rhododendrons or parched petunias. I told her that I thought she loved plants more than she loved me," Fern stared at her feet, "and that I didn't know why they'd even bothered having a kid." For months Fern had been afraid to speak these thoughts out loud. "Do you think she ran away because of me?"

Grandmamma looked at her granddaughter with one of those looks that adults give you when they're seeing into your heart.

"That's nonsense." She hugged Fern tight. "You mustn't think that way. Your mother loves you very deeply." But being told not to think that way and actually being able to not think that way are two different things. Fern imagined her mother saying, "How did I end up with such an ungrateful daughter? I think I'll go live with the sunflowers." She felt wretched, and she couldn't have cared less that the next day was her thirteenth birthday.

That night she lay in bed staring at her grandmother's fleur-de-lis wallpaper. Around the room hung framed photographs of Grandpapa Luc, who had died long ago, and of Olivier when he was a sweet-faced little boy. There was also a photo of grown-up

21

Olivier with Lily and baby Fern. Downstairs Fern heard her father describing his daughter with words like "depression," "guilt," and "therapy." Grandmamma's words—"time," "heal," and "love"—followed quickly behind. Fern strained to stay awake and listen. The bedside clock ticked rhythmically in her ear, and the minutes fell to the ground with hypnotic regularity. Fern nodded off, her cheek resting on the French lace pillow.

The Parisian moon shone through her window, the golden tips of the fleurs-de-lis sparkling in its beams. A warm breeze curled in through the room. It was very, very quiet. Except for one odd sound . . . a faint groaning. The groaning grew louder. Then, through the open window, a great green vine slowly slinked into the room like a giant python. The vine bumped into the picture frame that held the photo of Lily and Olivier holding newborn baby Fern. The picture fell to the floor with a crash. Fern woke up and sat bolt upright in her bed. The vine paused for a moment, as though gathering its wits, and then continued inching its way up to the seam connecting the ceiling to the walls. Fern stared at it, wide-eyed. She tried to call for help, but her lips felt glued together. The vine moved along one seam, then another and another, until it wound its way around the room, covering all four seams like a thick green rope. Fern sat dumbstruck, unable to move.

Enormous leaves sprouted from the vine's girth. Fern shrank back under the comforter. The vine groaned louder. The leaves pushed into the ceiling. Fern wondered why her father couldn't hear the noise. Then a thunderous explosion blew the entire roof off the room. Fern watched in shock as the ceiling floated up and away into the jet-black night sky. The golden fleurs-de-lis wriggled free from their wallpaper home, hovered briefly in the room like hummingbirds, and then waltzed upward, glowing as they drifted off.

Fern looked down and discovered her bed was now held aloft by a sturdy stand of palm trees. When she tried to scream, she couldn't open her mouth. She closed her eyes. When she opened them again, the palms had disappeared, replaced by a thick bed of seaweed that slapped the underbelly of the bed, keeping it afloat in an endless shimmering turquoise ocean. Fern dipped her finger in the water. It was as warm as soup. In the distance dolphins pirouetted above the waves like ballerinas. She blinked . . . and it was all gone. Now the bed was nestled in a field of fragrant lavender that rose waist high. A breeze blew across it, forming patterns in the blooms.

Fern's hair swirled around her head in the wind. A soft sound wafted toward her. Somewhere out in the distance she heard words. They were very faint. They seemed to be passed along by the swaying purplish plants. Fern listened hard. The words danced across the lavender, becoming clearer and clearer.

"Fern?" A voice called to her. All the color left Fern's face. While she didn't recognize the sound of the voice at all, it somehow felt like it was Lily speaking. "Can you hear me, Fern?" Fern frantically searched the field of lavender. "I'll come home as soon as I can. I promise!"

"Mom!!!!!" Fern cried out at the top of her lungs. "Mom! Where are you????" In an instant, the roof was back on the room and the fleurs-de-lis were back on the walls. Fern was sitting up in her bed, and Olivier and Grandmamma were hovering over her.

"It was a nightmare," Grandmamma shushed as she held a damp cloth to Fern's forehead. Olivier pressed a glass of cold water to her lips. It took a moment for Fern to get her bearings.

"Only a nightmare," repeated Olivier, hugging her. Fern looked into their extremely worried faces, and decided it was best to keep her dream or vision or whatever it really was to herself. It would only worry them more.

"Just a nightmare," Fern sighed. She drank some water and burrowed back under the comforter.

Grandmamma kissed her on her forehead. On his way out, Olivier retrieved the framed photo of him and his wife and their baby Fern from where it had inexplicably fallen. He turned off the light and closed the door.

"I heard you, Mom," Fern whispered out into the darkness.

The next morning was Fern's thirteenth birthday. She woke up feeling peculiarly refreshed. Her father entered her room and sang "Happy Birthday." He wrapped his arms around her in a huge hug. Grandmamma arrived with hot chocolate and beautiful, buttery madeleine cookies. Both of them watched Fern closely, as though they were afraid she might shatter.

"We have big plans for your birthday, *mon petit chou*," said Grandmamma.

"What are we waiting for?" Fern hopped out of bed. Olivier and Grandmamma exchanged a concerned look.

"Denial," Olivier whispered to his mother.

That day the three of them did a million things together. They went up the Eiffel Tower and had birthday cake and champagne on a boat on the Seine. They went to the Louvre Museum, saw a puppet show at the Luxembourg Gardens, and shopped at Galeries Lafayette. Grandmamma insisted on buying Fern many beautiful outfits that were neither ill fitting nor organic. She bought dresses and purses and jeans; an entire wardrobe of things that Fern had only seen in magazines. At the end of the day they went to the circus. They had done everything a person could do in Paris, all in one day. Fern knew what they were up to. If you keep someone very busy, they may forget what's bothering them. Grandmamma and Olivier didn't realize Fern was quite content, because in her heart of hearts she knew her mother would soon return home.

That evening, Olivier came up to say good night. He asked Fern if she'd had a good birthday. Fern knew that the unspoken end to that sentence was "a good birthday considering your mother has disappeared off the face of the planet."

Fern hugged Olivier. "I had a great birthday, Dad, but I really don't want to miss much more school. We should be getting back to Nedlaw soon." Fern was relieved when Olivier agreed with her. After all, what if Lily returned home while they were away in Paris?

A week later Olivier and Fern boarded a 747 from Paris for home. On board, Olivier thumbed his way through the most recent *American Fern Journal,* and came upon a picture of his beloved Lily in the "Missing Botanists" section. Fern watched her dad sadly close the magazine. She put her hand in her father's. He smiled at her and then sighed heavily, closed his eyes, and fell asleep. Fern took the *Journal* and tucked it in her shoulder bag.

When Olivier had believed his wife might be out there in the world, he couldn't sleep at all for waiting for her. Now that he thought she was never coming home, he could barely keep his eyes open. He had given up. Fern looked out through the shreds of white clouds down to the blue, blue ocean below. She recognized it was a different blue from the ocean of her dream. This ocean was a cold blue, but her dream ocean was warm. She knew that wherever that dream ocean was, that was where she would find her mother.

The Prisoner

Halfway around the world there's a lush green island that lingers just out to sea from a huge subcontinent. It's called Sri Lanka. Tigers and elephants roam its jungles. Blue-black bats sleep in towering trees, like tears of tar dripping from the limbs. Warm waves kiss the island's golden shores. On this island known for its rich vegetation and magnificent gems, in a deep, dank cave, lay Lily Verdant. Her eyes were closed. She lay on a bed covered with colorful cotton blankets. A plastic tube trailed from her arm up to an intravenous feeding device. Lily wasn't awake, and she hadn't been awake for six months. Nearby, on a small table equipped with a grow light, the Silver Rose watched over the sleeping Lily. It had been a long journey for the two of them.

The fateful night at the Hubris estate was the last time Lily had been conscious. As she plunged toward the sandy beach, the final thought to pass through her mind was *The gift! I must tell Fern about the gift.* The shock of the fall was traumatic for the Silver Rose. One of its petals fell off in the sand. A rush of cold water shuddered up the beach. The single silver petal was pulled out to sea on icy waves.

"I don't like this," Luella said when the unconscious Lily was brought back to the mansion. Luella had several reasons to be annoyed by the situation. Among them was the streak of green jealousy flowing through her veins. She hated having a sleeping beauty under her roof.

Beneath the mansion, behind a wine cellar where many bottles of Château d'Hubris lay carefully stored, was a secret room with a hidden entrance. This is where Claude and Luella hid Lily when the police arrived to search for her. This is where Lily lay when Fern and Olivier arrived at the Hubris mansion. Lily could hear their voices above her. She heard their footsteps on the carefully polished oak floor. But she could not open her eyes, or call to them. In her head she was screaming out their names, but only a slight whoosh of air escaped her lips, and a single tear escaped her eye.

By the time the authorities had arrived, Luella had cosmetically repaired the Silver Rose. To the layperson, the Silver Rose looked fine. The detectives couldn't detect its prosthetic petal. Olivier's despair clouded his botanical judgment. There was no reason for anyone to believe that foul play was responsible for Lily's disappearance.

After Fern and Olivier left, Claude and Luella began bickering about their course of action. The shrill ring of the telephone interrupted them. Claude picked it up.

"Hello?" He was expecting another inquiry from the police or those irritating Verdants. But it was someone else, someone whose very voice caused Claude's mouth to turn dry and his eyes to open wide.

"Ugghhh, hello . . . Mr. Saagwalla." Claude did not sound like his usual smooth and confident self. "Yes, we do have her. But you see . . . there's been a bit of a hiccup." Claude went on to explain that the "hiccup" was a comatose botanist. He held the phone away from his ear as words exploded out of the receiver. Luella's face turned whiter than usual. Her rabbit stole fled from her shoulders, the yellow fur creating a mustard blur as it escaped from the room.

"Immediately," Claude said. But the phone line was already dead. Claude's whole body shook as he called out for the Chia Man.

"Pack up everything!" Claude yelled to his leafy servant. "We're leaving."

Very early the next morning, in a yacht with the golden symbols $$$$$$$ scrawled on its sides, Claude, Luella, an unconscious Lily, a distressed Silver Rose, and a green-headed man sailed away. They left behind a completely empty mansion. Not even a single bottle of Château d'Hubris remained. It was as if no one had ever been there.

The $$$$$$$ was a very fancy yacht, and Luella and Claude spent the long days sailing across the ocean playing shuffleboard and sipping martinis. Lily and the Silver Rose were sequestered below deck. They moved west, and the sea became warmer. The $$$$$$ came upon a bed of thick seaweed that stretched for miles. As the slippery slabs slapped at the boat's underbelly, the seaweed intuited that there was a very special cargo on this boat. Luella looked overboard.

"That noise is really irritating," she said to herself. "Someone should hack the tops off that seaweed." The seaweed saw Luella's face leaning over the side of the yacht and shrank away from the hull. In their berth below deck, both Lily and the Silver Rose sensed the seaweed's presence. Lily's eyelids flickered.

After sailing halfway around the world, the yacht entered a cove fringed with large, drooping palm trees. The weather was warm, and the sand was almost white. The yacht moored, and from there Lily and the Rose were taken to a secret cave where Claude and Luella kept constant vigil over them.

"She better be conscious by the time he gets here," said Claude.

"And exactly how are we supposed to accomplish that?" Luella snapped.

Claude didn't have a clue. He flew in doctors from around the world, the kind of doctors who could be trusted not to report a comatose missing botanist to the police. Claude paid them handsomely to find out when Lily might awaken, but not one of them had the answer.

"This is ridiculous," Luella whined. "Isn't there something you can do? How long can a person stay in a coma?" Luella paced back and forth in the cave. Chia Man listened nearby.

"Thirty-seven years, one hundred and eleven days," answered Claude, "according to the *Guinness Book of World Records*." The Rose listened intently to the conversation.

"Well, I am not going to wait thirty-seven years and one hundred and eleven days," snapped Luella.

"No, indeed." Claude loomed over Lily, willing her eyes to open, his tanned skin shiny in the cave-light. "What we want is in that lovely brain."

"Did you say 'lovely'?" Luella narrowed her eyes jealously. She hated it when Claude looked at any other woman, even one in a coma.

"Henry Saagwalla will know what to do," said Claude. Luella shut up. The python belt circling her hips dropped to the ground and fled into a gloomy corner. Neither Hubris nor accessory was looking forward to the arrival of their boss.

Lily was unconscious and couldn't speak, but she could hear. She had been confident that an avenue of escape would present itself right up until she heard Claude Hubris say the name "Henry Saagwalla." Fear flowed through her veins.

Of course, thought Lily, remembering the monogrammed HS on the towel back at the Hubris mansion. *Henry Saagwalla is behind this!* Lily knew she was running out of time. She had to contact Fern immediately. There was some very important information she needed to pass along to her daughter, and Lily knew that once Henry Saagwalla got hold of her, she might never have the opportunity.

Home Again

Olivier had worried that returning home might have some dark effect on Fern. Remarkably, she seemed peculiarly well adjusted. Fern didn't tell her father about her dream. It felt like something private that she should keep close to her heart. Besides, Olivier would say it was only a nightmare, or he'd call Grandmamma, and they would talk about "therapy." So Fern kept quiet. Every night she went to bed hoping her mother might contact her again.

Things were very different when Fern Verdant returned to eighth grade. In her brand-new stylish French wardrobe, she was the best-dressed girl at Joan Baez Middle School. Lily's disappearance had taken on a life of its own. When it first happened, all anyone could say was "I'm sorry." They were afraid to look into Fern's eyes. But now Lily's disappearance had been transformed from an uncomfortable tragedy into an exotic enigma. Fern had become a well-dressed girl accessorized by a mystery.

The popular girls at school decided that Fern might be a good addition to their clique. Lily's disappearance would lend them an air of romantic tragedy, and more importantly, Fern had a French grandmother who might be persuaded to send them designer cheerleading costumes from Paris. Fern had lost her mother, but found Brittany, Emily, and Alicia. It had been a long time since she'd had a friend, and she welcomed the distraction.

Brittany, Emily, and Alicia were concerned with three things: boys, clothes, and the cheerleading squad. The girls helped Fern straighten her hair and taught her how to use lip gloss correctly. They took her to a football practice of the Baez Bulldogs. Fern knew that if her mother were here, she would have disapproved of these gossipy girls. She also knew that if her mother were real instead of a mystery, Brittany, Emily, and Alicia would have had nothing to do with her.

One afternoon, when she and the girls were in her room talking, Fern heard the oddest sound. It was a squeaky little voice.

"Ouch," it said.

"What was that?" asked Fern.

"What was what?" asked Brittany, Emily, and Alicia in unison.

"You didn't hear an *ouch*?"

"An *ouch*?" asked Emily, puzzled.

"I think your Tangerine Twist toenail polish went to your

head," said Brittany. "It's dead quiet here. We're out in the middle of, like, nowhere."

"Yeah, like, miles from the nearest Starbucks," whined Alicia.

Fern was sure she'd heard an "Ouch," but she didn't press the issue. These girls were very quick to criticize, and could be quite mean. Fern was not in the mood for mean.

Later, after the girls had left, Fern noticed that the seed her mother had given her, the seed that had been dormant for so long, had sprouted several inches since that morning. *How peculiar*, she thought.

Fern lay down. The next thing she knew she'd drifted off into one of those late-afternoon naps where the dreams are strangely vivid. The kind of dreams that seem so real, if you were dreaming about escaping from a giant shark, you might wake up to find your feet thrashing about at the foot of your bed.

In Fern's dream the seed suddenly shot up. It grew so tall that it loomed above her like a tree or the Eiffel Tower. There was a loud popping sound, and a bud sprouted on the end of the stalk. The bud grew larger, unfurling into a flower the shape of a giant white cone, or a megaphone. It was enormous. The flower bent down toward Fern. It enveloped her entirely, and shouted one word.

"LISTEN!"

Fern woke up with a start, nearly falling off the bed. She clasped her hands over her ears. The seed had grown an additional eight inches during her nap. As she watched it, the flower unfurled, faster than any flower should. What on earth

34

was happening? Fern jumped out of bed and bolted from her room to find her father. Olivier looked up when Fern entered the greenhouse. She was shaky and anxious. She sat in the chair next to him and rested her head against his shoulder.

"I feel like something very peculiar is happening."

"Peculiar in what way?" Olivier asked, hoping she might finally share her feelings.

Fern looked at Olivier. She loved her father, but could she tell him about her strange dreams, about the plant in her room, or about the "ouch" voice in her head? He was a scientific man. He'd think she was crazy.

"Oh . . . it's nothing," she sighed. "I'm being silly." She kissed Olivier and went upstairs.

The next day Fern went to school as usual. She tried to put the screaming plant out of her head. This was the day of the Joan Baez Bulldogs cheerleading tryout. Brittany, Emily, and Alicia insisted that Fern try out for a newly opened spot. Brittany had "accidentally" tripped cheerleader Courtney Lawson, who had broken her ankle, leaving a vacancy on the squad. Brittany, Emily, and Alicia had coached Fern, who felt quite awkward during practice. The girls insisted she was a natural. At the end of the school day, five candidates stood ready to give the Baez Bulldog cheer.

The bleachers were packed with kids. The Bulldogs themselves were there. Girls watched because they wanted to be like the cheerleaders, and boys watched because they thought the girls were cute. Fern felt very self-conscious. She'd never had football players notice her before.

One by one the candidates performed their cheers. The audience sniggered and booed after a bad performance and cheered after a good one. Petrified, Fern waited for her turn. Brittany, Emily, and Alicia made sure she went last so that her cheers would be fresh in everyone's minds. The trio had mentioned to the judges how fabulous the squad would look in designer French uniforms. Fern walked out onto the field across the stubbly greens.

"*Ouch, ouch, ouch,*" squeaked out from somewhere underfoot. The sound was faint and barely perceptible. Fern paused for a moment, not sure if she'd heard it at all. Everyone was watching her. She continued out to a patch of grass that was the audition area. Brittany, Emily, and Alicia stood with their fingers crossed, discussing the merits of plum versus vermilion uniforms. Fern took her position, clutching her pom-poms to her chest. She cleared her throat and looked out at the crowd, which was anxiously waiting to tear her apart or cheer her on. It was dead quiet. Fern nervously shouted out the school cheer.

Crush them, beat them,
Bury them in the ground.
Bulldogs! Bulldogs!
The best all around.
Break their arms,
Break their legs,
They are the losers!
They are the dregs!

The onlookers cheered wildly. It was time for Fern to begin the athletic portion of her cheer. She crouched down into a squat, readying for her first leap into the air. She shook the pom-poms wildly in her hand, then she vaulted. It was magnificent. She leapt four feet into the air, her arms spread out wide, as if she were embracing the world. She looked out at the crowd of spectators, and could see the approval in their eyes. It seemed like the most perfect moment in the world. The past year had been so difficult. But at this instant, as she floated above the football field of Joan Baez Middle School, everyone watching her proudly, life was excellent.

Then she thumped back to earth, and everything changed. The moment her feet hit the ground, she was nearly deafened by the loudest, most painful, earsplitting scream.

"OOUUCCHH!!!"

It was so loud that Fern dropped her pom-poms, covered her ears, and fell to the ground. A surge of voices vied for attention in her head.

"What do you think you're doing?" one voice yelled at her.

"Get off of us, you big oaf!" shrieked another.

"What do you think this is, a trampoline?" gagged a third.

"Help us!" They all cried together.

Fern stared wild-eyed at the ground. The voices were coming from the blades of grass beneath her, blades that looked like perfectly normal grass, just a little crushed from where she'd landed. She leapt up as if the blades were hot coals. She sprinted toward an earthy area of the field, the voices calling after her.

"That's better," cried one voice.

"Watch where you're going next time," shouted another voice.

Confused, Fern called back to the grassy patch.

"I don't understand what's happening to me. Am I going crazy?" And she started to cry.

One sympathetic blade of grass, sounding a little older than the others, said, "There, there, dear. Someone really should explain things to you."

Fern began to sob out loud. When she looked up, she saw the crowd that mere moments ago had been gazing at her with pride was now staring at her with curiosity, and even fear. They had the same expression in their eyes that Grandmamma and Olivier had had in Paris, the kind of look people give you when they're afraid you might shatter. Fueled by nerves, the crowd started to snigger, one by one. The sniggers grew into giggles that grew into guffaws. The entire football team erupted in howls of laughter. Chased by this wall of laughter, Fern ran off the field to the bus stop, where she caught the first bus home to Olivier.

Brittany, Emily, and Alicia agreed that French fashion was overrated, and too avant-garde, anyway. They acknowledged that they'd been foolish to put their valuable support behind such a total loser.

An Explanation

Fern arrived home a complete mess. Her eyes were red from crying, and she was covered in grass stains. She ran to the greenhouse. Olivier gave her a big hug.

"Fern, you look terrible. What happened?"

"Dad," Fern said, shaking. She was trying to figure out where to start. She took a big breath.

"Weird things have been happening to me lately."

"What kind of weird things?" asked Olivier, concerned.

"I know this is going to sound strange, but sometimes . . . I hear things. I hear—"

"Noooooooooooooooo!!!!!!!!!!!!!!!!!!!!!!!!!"

The word shot into her head like a bullet. Fern shut her eyes tightly and put her hands over her ears, which didn't help because the voice was coming from inside her head. Olivier hadn't heard a thing, and he was startled by his daughter's behavior.

"What on earth is happening to you?" Olivier asked.

Once again the voice in her head shouted. This time it said, "Red alert! Red alert! Do not tell him. I repeat . . . you must not tell him!!!! Come to your room immediately!"

The voice sounded vaguely familiar to Fern. Could it be . . . was it possibly the talking plant from her dream?

"It's a matter of your mother's life and death."

Fern's face went white. Olivier looked at her with renewed concern.

"Dad," she cried, "I have an awful headache." She put her hand on her stomach. "I mean an awful stomachache." She put her hand to her forehead. "I . . . I've just had a terrible day. I really just need to rest."

Fern kissed her father on the cheek, and walked out of the greenhouse. Once out of his sight, she ran up the stairs as if crocodiles were snapping at her heels, leaving behind a very bewildered and concerned parent.

In her room, she found the plant exactly where she'd left it, in its pot by her bedside—except now it stood a foot tall.

"Who are you? Why are you tormenting me?" Fern demanded.

Silence.

"*Now* you're not speaking to me?"

"Not if you're going to shout!" the plant said irritably.

Fern stepped back, shocked. A houseplant had just spoken

to her. Well, not exactly "spoken"; its thoughts were projected directly into Fern's head.

"I'm sorry. I'm not usually so rude, but this has been a weird day . . . and . . . you're a plant?"

"To be specific, I'm a Trumpet Flower. Ash-leaved."

"Why are you talking to me? What has this got to do with my mother?"

"Oh . . . I have so many things to tell you. I'm already exhausted and I haven't even begun." Fern listened, dumbfounded. "I have news from your mother . . ."

"Is she all right?" Fern interrupted.

"Well . . . sort of . . . it's complicated. Your mother sent this message to explain everything to you. The message was passed from a rose to moss to weeds to flowers to trees to me. We're like botanical e-mail . . . and yes, we know what the Internet is. Just because we're pretty doesn't mean we're stupid. Houseplants can be particularly observant. After all, there is only so much television you can watch. I don't know how you people do it!

"Your mother wants you to know something . . . something very important. In case you haven't figured it out yet, you have a fantastic gift. You can communicate with plants and they can communicate with you."

Fern's mouth fell open.

"Your mother has the same gift. So did your mother's mother, and her mother, and so on. No one knows how or why. But she knew you'd get the gift when you turned thirteen, just like she did."

41

"But . . . but . . . but . . . !!!!" Fern didn't even know what to say.

The Trumpet Flower continued on. "It's a complicated gift, as many gifts are, but one important aspect of it is that you cannot tell anyone in the whole world you have it . . . because the minute you do—the second the words escape your mouth—it will disappear. Your father doesn't even know."

A flood of thoughts rushed through Fern's head. First and foremost was how ridiculous it was that a girl who hated plants should inherit the gift of communicating with them. Right now, she felt like yelling at them all. Plants had given her her stupid name, made the family move to Nedlaw, and taken her mother away. Fern despised plants.

"The gift develops in fits and starts," the Trumpet Flower continued. "Usually there is a mother involved to guide you through it. This gift is why your mother traveled around the world. Even though it broke her heart to leave you, she could hear the painful cries of dying species. She had to respond. Your mother says that if you listen hard, you can even hear the growing pains of plants as they inch up to the sunlight, which she says is a strangely wonderful thing.

"You'll notice that you spoke with me by mouth . . . so quaint, but also very unsanitary. Did you know a human's mouth has more bacteria than a dog's? Ugh! Eventually you will grow into your gift and develop the focus required to speak with plants telepathically. It may take a little time . . . always does, but don't worry, it'll happen, maybe when you least expect it."

"Wait a minute! Why are you telling me all of this when my mom will explain everything when she returns?"

The Flower was uncomfortably quiet.

"Well?" Fern prodded.

"Things have taken an unforeseen turn for the worse. Your mother is being held prisoner by the really rotten Hubrises. They work for a particularly evil man named Henry Saagwalla, who ordered your mother's kidnapping for some despicable and unknown reason. I'm delivering this message because she's been delayed. Actually, she is in a coma. She can think, but she can't move or open her eyes or escape. Your mother heard you upstairs at the Hubris mansion. She was a prisoner in the wine cellar, and unable to answer you. She wants you to know how deeply she loves you. She asks that you use your gift wisely and well, for it is a remarkable blessing."

"But I had a dream and in it my mother told me she was coming home!"

"That was before she learned Henry Saagwalla was involved."

"Henry Saagwalla?"

"A truly treacherous man." The Trumpet Flower shuddered at the thought.

"Can you at least tell me where she is?"

"I really don't know where she is. Your mother loves you too much to put you in danger. The Silver Rose that sent this message was given strict instructions not to reveal their whereabouts. Your mother helped the Silver Rose and it would never betray her wishes. You must look after your father and carry on the work."

Fern was quiet. The Trumpet Flower was unsure what to say next. This was the end of its instructions.

"I'll answer any questions I can." The Flower was feeling a little awkward. "But I only know what was passed along by the Willow."

"The Willow?" asked Fern.

"The message came from the Weeping Willow outside your window."

Fern looked out and saw the Willow's elegant long branches brush against the windowpane. This whole situation was very strange.

Fern was trying to make sense of everything. She was relieved to learn her mother was still alive. There was no question in her mind what she must do; she had to find her mother! But where on earth would she begin? Who could help her? Should she go to her father or to the police? What would she tell them? "I know my mother is alive somewhere in the world because a house-plant told me!" Any mention of this to her father and she'd lose her gift—and probably the only way she had to find her mom. Would anyone believe her anyway? It was all too confusing.

Fern had a headache from thinking too much. The Flower was asleep. Outside, the sun was turning a violent pink as it inched toward the horizon. Fern heard Olivier coming up the stairs to check on her. She quickly crawled under the covers and pretended she was in a deep sleep. She was afraid that she might blurt out the whole story and ruin everything.

Olivier tiptoed into Fern's room. He gently stroked her forehead and whispered "poor lamb," then kissed her and left. As soon as he was gone, Fern's eyes popped open. Several hours earlier she had been horribly upset by the cheerleading catastrophe; now she could barely remember it. It seemed like the most unimportant thing in the world.

The Weeping Willow's branches chattered against one another in the wind, sounding like clicking tongues. Fern sat on the edge of her bed and looked at the tree, a link in the relay of her mother's message. It had stood by her window since they'd moved into the house, but she had barely noticed it. That tree might be full of information.

Closing her eyes and feeling a little self-conscious, she thought the words *Willow-willow-willow-willow*. She repeated the words over and over like a mantra, but she couldn't get rid of the other thoughts crowding into her head. *Was her mother really okay? Why had her family been given this gift? How long had they had it? Could all plants communicate with humans? If plants could communicate, then could animals too?* Every time she had a clear thought of the tree, the other thoughts barged into her brain.

A Decision

Dawn found Fern staring at her computer screen, shocked. The name Henry Saagwalla loomed on the monitor in front of her. She discovered he was a very rich man who had been horribly scarred in a childhood incident. He owned gold mines in South Africa, copper mines in Papua, New Guinea, rubber plantations in Brazil, and oil fields in the Arctic. Everything he did to make money destroyed nature. He ruined forests, polluted waters, destroyed landscapes, and extinguished ecosystems. What could such an evil man want with a woman whose purpose in life was to save plants?

Fern stared out at the Willow. She hadn't slept one minute all night for thinking and plotting. She realized there was no one she could turn to for help. If people asked her how she knew her mother was alive, and where she was, Fern would have to

46

answer "A flower told me, but it's keeping the location secret per my mother's unconscious wishes."

But if Lily's words had wound their way around the globe by blades and leaves and flowers and weeds and moss, then perhaps there was a trail leading back to her, like leafy breadcrumbs. This, Fern decided, was how she would use her gift. She would trace the message all the way back to the Silver Rose and her mother.

It was very early in the morning, and a sepia light was beginning to coat the world with warmth. Fern crept outside. She walked to the Weeping Willow, feeling a little strange. It was one thing to chat with a plant in the privacy of your own room, but quite another to be standing outside in soon-to-be broad daylight, beginning a conversation with a tree. Fern looked around to make sure she was alone. She cleared her throat.

"Um . . . excuse me, but do you know where my mother is?" Fern whispered, feeling self-conscious.

The tree was silent. Fern stared at it expectantly.

"Where . . . is . . . my . . . mother?" Fern repeated loudly and slowly, like someone visiting a foreign country who doesn't speak the local language. Then she added, "Please."

Nothing.

"Perhaps you could tell me which plant passed the message to you, maybe just point your branches in its general direction?"

Silence.

"I'm new at this, and maybe I'm doing something wrong, but could you give me a break? This is very important!"

Fern was losing her patience.

* * *

Back in the house, Olivier had just woken up. He threw on his bathrobe and headed toward the stairs and his first cup of café au lait of the day. As he passed a large window, out of the corner of his eye, he saw his daughter talking to a tree. Olivier quietly slid open the window.

Fern was standing with her hands on her hips, shouting, "Where is my mother?"

Olivier's mouth dropped open.

"Why won't you answer me?" Fern was frustrated and angry. "Something terrible could happen to her, then how would you feel?"

She glanced down. She noticed a scar on the tree's trunk.

"Oh, no!" Fern gasped. She ran her hand along the gouged bark of the Willow, realizing that the wound had been caused by the pot of soil she'd hurled out of her window the night before her mother went away.

"Oh, no! I'm so sorry. No wonder you're not talking to me."

In the window above her, Olivier's face transformed from that of a man who had just woken up, eager for his coffee, to that of a man who was frightened for the mental health of his daughter. Olivier hid behind the curtains. Fern went back in the house, afraid she would never be able to get the Willow to speak with her.

Olivier had to wait three hours until the office of Dr. Marita Von Svenson, a psychiatrist at NITPIC, the Nedlaw Institute for the Treatment and Prevention of Insanity in Children, opened for business. He made an emergency appointment,

48

explaining that his daughter was inching away from sanity. Olivier informed Dr. Marita Von Svenson that Fern's mother had drowned near a particularly rugged area of the northwest coastline of Oregon, on a gray and horrid day in March. He acknowledged that as a botanist he knew the value of speaking to plants, but this was different. His daughter expected them to answer.

An hour later Olivier enlisted Fern to come into Nedlaw with him to run some errands. En route he explained that they were really going to visit Dr. Marita Von Svenson; that it would be good for Fern to have someone to talk to.

"I don't need someone to talk to!"

But Olivier insisted. When Fern entered Dr. Von Svenson's office, Olivier tried to follow, but the doctor's shapely secretary, Beatrice Minx, made him stay in the waiting area.

Everything in Dr. Marita Von Svenson's office was made of leather. Fern sat on a big leather couch in front of a bookcase filled with leather-bound books. The psychiatrist sat across from her in a leather chair, wearing a leather suit. She wore black-rimmed glasses and looked very serious. Her white blond hair was swept up in a chignon, and held in place by a Freudian clip. Fern couldn't tell how old she was because she didn't have a single line on her face. This was because she rarely showed an emotion.

"How are you feeling, Fern?" she asked in a thick Swedish accent.

"Okay," answered Fern, wondering why she was here at all.

"Okay?" asked Dr. Von Svenson.

"Okay," answered Fern.

"Hmmmmm." Dr. Von Svenson began scribbling notes. "Really?"

"Yes," Fern answered.

"Nothing you'd like to talk about?" asked the doctor.

"Nothing." Fern kicked her feet against the couch nervously. Dr. Von Svenson looked at them and said, "Hmmmm." She then made several more notes before continuing. Fern felt like a bug under a microscope.

"You're sure you wouldn't like to discuss the conversation you were having with a weeping willow tree on your lawn this morning at five-forty-five a.m. Pacific Daylight Time?"

Fern's face went white. She didn't know her father had seen her talking to the tree. Dr. Von Svenson noticed the panic in the girl's eyes, and stared at Fern even harder.

"I don't know what you're talking about." Fern tried to keep the shaking out of her voice.

"Sometimes we can animate inanimate objects in our head. We can give them human characteristics, out of superstition or fear. After all, you've been through a traumatic time these last months."

Fern said nothing. Dr. Von Svenson leaned forward to within inches of her face.

"Did the tree answer you?"

Fern looked away, determined not to speak. They both sat stubbornly and awkwardly silent for twenty minutes.

"This session's over." The doctor tried to keep the irritation out of her voice. Fern was so nervous that her legs had gotten sweaty and stuck to the leather couch. She pried herself off the sofa and ran to the bathroom, where she splashed cold water on her hot face. Outside she overheard Dr. Von Svenson and her father talking.

"Shut down. Denial. Alienated. Withdrawn," said Von Svenson.

"I think your daughter should be an in-patient. We could monitor her properly if she lived at the NITPIC facility."

"But it's been a very difficult year, and I think we should be together."

The doctor looked at Olivier. "Don't you want her to get well?"

"Of course I do."

"Grief is a powerful thing. If she was under my constant supervision, I'm sure I could help her get through this."

Later, in the car, Olivier asked his daughter how she had liked Dr. Marita Von Svenson.

"Not at all," Fern answered. She stared silently out the window all the way home. When they arrived there, Fern raced up to her room, slamming the door behind her.

"I have an emergency. Wake up!" She shook the pot by her bed.

"Get ahold of yourself!" The Trumpet Flower was half-awake. "Where's the fire?"

"Sorry. My father took me to a psychiatrist. She wants me to talk about 'everything.' I'm worried I'll blurt it all out."

"A psychiatrist?" asked the Trumpet Flower.

"If you're not normal, they make you talk until you become normal."

"Of course you're not normal," the Trumpet Flower laughed. "You're very special. You have a gift. You must tell the tree what you've just told me. It's still angry with you, but perhaps if you explain the situation thoroughly?"

Fern checked to make sure her father was in the greenhouse, and not spying on her. Then she went outside to the wounded Willow.

"Weeping Willow, I beg you to help me. If someone threw a pot of soil and scarred me, I'd be mad too, but I really need your help. Desperately. A psychiatrist is trying to make me talk! I could lose the gift! Please, it's important. Tell me who gave you the message from my mother."

The tree stood mutely.

"If something were to happen to her, or to me, then there would be no one who can hear plants cry for help!"

Silence.

"You'd have no friends in the whole world," Fern continued.

Fern heard something that sounded like the clearing of a throat, and then a lilting female voice exclaimed, in a slight Southern accent, "With friends like you, who needs enemies!"

"Thank you!" Fern sighed with relief. "Thank you so much for speaking to me!"

"You don't know how lucky you are that I am talking to you, darling. You cannot begin to imagine the pain I have suffered on account of your most vicious attack. Look at me! I was considered a beauty—now I'm scarred for life!" The Weeping Willow actually sounded as though it was weeping. Fern felt horrible.

"Your scar is barely noticeable."

"Only someone very young would say such a thing," the tree sighed.

"I'm sorry . . . but please, this is really important! I must find out where my mother's message came from!"

The Willow cleared its throat for dramatic effect. "I received your mother's message from a Fir tree, about a hundred miles due south of here in a town called Dimple-by-the-Sea. That tree's voice made my leaves flutter. Strong. Sure. I suspect his roots might be Yankee."

"Did the Fir in Dimple-by-the-Sea say anything else? Did he say which plants passed my mother's message along? Did he say where they were?"

For a moment there was only the sound of the Willow's branches rustling and whispering against one another as a breeze floated through the leaves.

"I'm sorry . . . I don't know who sent the message to the Fir. I only know it was that strong, masculine, probably very handsome tree that passed it on to me."

Fern cleared her throat, returning the Willow to the subject at hand. "Do you have any idea where my mother is?"

"No. I'm sorry, I don't."

"Maybe the Fir tree knows. Could you contact him for me?"

"I do not possess the ability to send a message that far. Some voices are stronger than others, my dear. I happen to be quite delicate and feminine, with a soft voice and a limited range."

53

Fern had a sinking feeling. Was she going to have to trace back her mother's message, plant by temperamental plant, all the way to the source?

The Willow made a shuddery sound. "Do you ever get the creepy feeling you're being watched?" Fern looked up just in time to see Olivier's head disappear into her bedroom window. He had come to check up on her. He looked out of her window, and saw what he feared the most, his daughter having an animated conversation with a tree. In a flash he was outside, and hugging her.

"I'm at my wits' end," Olivier said.

Fern said nothing for fear of saying too much.

"I love you more than anything, and I'll do whatever it takes to help you get better. I think it would be best if you spent some time at NITPIC. Dr. Marita Von Svenson will be able to help you get better."

"Dad, there's nothing wrong with me!" cried Fern.

"I saw you talking to that tree again."

"But you talk to your plants all the time!"

"That's different. Your mother is . . . gone. You were asking a tree where she was and expecting an answer."

"Please don't send me to NITPIC."

"It is the finest institute of its kind. They'll help you. I love you too much to lose you as well. Now go and pack some things."

Olivier went to phone Dr. Marita Von Svenson. He felt terrible, but he didn't know what else to do. Fern returned her attention to the Willow.

"Thank you for your help," she whispered. "I think you are beautiful, and I will be sure to tell that to the Fir tree when I meet it . . . which I think is going to be very soon."

Fern went inside, knowing that this would be the last day she spent in her own house for a very long time. But she had no idea just how long it would be.

The Great Escape

Fern didn't need to pack too much since NITPIC patients wore uniforms and really didn't have use for much clothing. But she did fill her backpack for another journey. Fern had often watched her mother pack for her trips, so she knew just how to pack and what to take. Lily always sealed her belongings in ziplock bags to protect them against the elements. Fern did the same. First and foremost she packed her mother's *Dictionary of International Botany*. Lily's name was inscribed on the first page. She took a pocket atlas, binoculars, a flashlight, sunglasses, and hiking boots. She packed some of the energy bars Lily always kept in the pantry. Her mother told her that they were the kind of thing you'd eat "if you and your yak were on top of a mountain peak, starving to bits." Each bar felt like it weighed fifty pounds. Fern also packed her entire life savings, three hundred twenty-two dollars and fifty-seven cents, which she kept hidden in an old sock pinned to the sleeve of her rain-coat.

Later that day a very glum Olivier drove a very glum Fern to NITPIC. Everything outside was gray. Father and daughter barely spoke. Olivier was wondering if he was doing the right thing. Fern was wondering what the future would hold. They entered a long driveway. On either side the lawn was manicured within an inch of its life. Every blade of grass was exactly the same height. Security guards patrolled the grounds. Massive Douglas firs lined the drive. Fern wondered if they might be re-lated to the Fir tree in Dimple-by-the-Sea.

"Maybe you can help me?" she whispered out to them as the Verdant vehicle drove past.

"Did you say something?" Olivier asked.

"Nothing," replied Fern, staring out the window.

Fern looked with dread at the big brick building that was NITPIC. It was a hundred years old, and was dark and heavy and sad. It was like a prison. Dr. Marita Von Svenson stood waiting for them on the front steps. She reminded Fern of a spi-der watching a fly enter her web. Fern walked up the steps toward the icy psychiatrist with only one thought on her mind: this woman would never prevent her from finding her mother.

"It's a beautiful lawn, isn't it?" said Dr. Marita Von Svenson. "Not a blade of grass out of place."

She took Olivier aside. "You've done the right thing, Mr. Verdant. We'll take care of her here. Now say goodbye. It's the last you'll see of her for a while, as we advise no visitation. It's part of the treatment. Too distracting to have parents popping in and out."

"But . . . but . . . ," Olivier stammered. "What about phone calls?"

"A few," Dr. Von Svenson said, "but only now and then."

A round ball of a man, Mr. Carruthers, was summoned to escort Fern to her room. He was furtive, with droplets of sweat that clung to his brow.

"Goodbye." Olivier hugged Fern, then reluctantly let her go.

Mr. Carruthers steered Fern inside, but she wriggled free of his damp clutches, racing to the open front door. She watched as Olivier drove slowly down the winding NITPIC driveway and thought about crying, but knew that wouldn't get her anywhere. She felt like an orphan; one parent was missing and the other had abandoned her. Olivier looked back over his shoulder as he drove away.

Huffing and puffing, Mr. Carruthers steered the struggling girl back through the massive wooden doors.

"Stop wriggling, my dear. Give yourself a chance. I really think that you'll be happy here." Dr. Marita Von Svenson leaned in so she was inches away from Fern's face. "And even if you're not, I don't care. Tomorrow we start . . . with hypnotherapy."

Fern struggled against Carruthers' grip. She knew what hypnotherapy was . . . she knew it could make you speak the truth no matter what. If Dr. Von Svenson hypnotized Fern, she would be forced to reveal her secret, and then she would lose it!

The front door of the institute slammed shut, and was bolted. Carruthers was now practically dragging her.

The corridors of the Nedlaw Institute for the Treatment and Prevention of Insanity in Children were white and sterile. Disoriented children roamed the halls like ghosts. Some cried at nothing, others laughed at nothing. Carruthers pushed Fern into her room. The windows were barred, the walls were stark, and a single lightbulb was suspended from the ceiling by a dangling wire. There was a little desk, with paper and a pencil on it, and a single bed. The room smelled like disinfectant.

"Don't forget to put on your uniform." Carruthers pointed to a baggy white jumpsuit that hung from a hook on the wall. NITPIC was printed across the back in giant black letters. Beside it was the NITPIC logo, a thick red circle surrounding the face of a screaming child, eyes wide and hair standing on end. A big red line was slashed across the face. Fern already hated NITPIC. It did not seem like a place where people regained their happiness.

"Bathroom and showers are down the hall to your left. Dinner is at six p.m. sharp." Carruthers shut the door behind him.

Fern took off her backpack and changed into the jumpsuit. Outside, the sky was dark, and clouds as black as panthers hovered just inches above the institute. Buckets of rain fell. The wind blew through the barred, open window. Fern looked out over the grounds and wondered if it was raining where her mother was. She thought back to the days when Lily was with them, and realized that she had been very lucky indeed. As Fern headed downstairs to the dining room, she did not see, in the hall, in the shadows, Dr. Marita Von Svenson creep quietly into her room.

The dining room contained rows and rows of long tables set with plastic spoons and plastic bowls. A hundred children filed in, all wearing the NITPIC overalls with the NITPIC logo. They acted like they were half-asleep. One boy stumbled and fell. He stayed lying on the ground until security personnel picked him up by the scruff of his jumpsuit and carried him out of the room. The children sat on benches and silently ate their bowls of curdled green stew. Fern noticed everyone's hair was cut quite short. She sat beside a girl about her own age, whose bright orange hair stuck out as if she'd put her finger in an electric socket. The girl stared at Fern's long ebony curls.

"Hello, I'm Fern."

The girl's mouth fell open in surprise, and her eyes darted about the room nervously. Several other children looked up, startled, before quickly diverting their attention back toward their meals.

"What's your name?"

"Francesca," the girl whispered, looking very guilty.

"Aren't we allowed to talk to each other?"

Francesca shook her head. "Whenever we speak, they twist and turn our words around. They use them against us to make us seem crazy. Then they give us more 'treatment.' "

"Treatment?"

Francesca nodded, wincing at a memory too awful for words.

"Can't you call your family and tell them?" Fern asked.

"My parents died when I was small. I had a twin brother, too, but they separated us." Francesca looked down sadly.

"Why would anyone do such a thing?"

Francesca shrugged. "I lived with a family when I was little, but I had an imaginary friend. The family brought me here and never came back for me. The institute gets money to look after crazy orphans. One day I'll leave here. If only I wasn't always so tired." Above them, hail the size of golf balls banged loudly on the roof.

"My brother's out there somewhere. He's going to find me. I know it. I got a letter from him once, but *she* took it away from me."

Fern was horrified! Imagine having a brother and two parents and losing them all. It was hard enough having a missing mother. Fern looked around. These children didn't seem like regular children in the least. They all looked exhausted and vacant in the exact same way. She suddenly felt queasy with the realization that it might not be easy to escape from here. Fern got up and hurried toward an exit.

"I don't feel very well!" she blurted out to a guard. Fern dashed through a set of doors to the bathroom, but the doors didn't lead to a bathroom, they led to the kitchen. A white-coated NITPIC employee stood in front of rows and rows of vials, each filled with a chalky liquid. The vials were emptied into endless jugs of milk. Fern read a label on one of the vials. In small print were the words *Permanently Exhausted*. A set of hard hands rested on her shoulders, and she turned to find herself looking up at Dr. Marita Von Svenson.

61

"The bathroom is this way." She steered Fern down a hallway. Fern didn't feel sick anymore, just frightened. Dr. Von Svenson waited for her, and escorted her to her bench in the dining hall. Back in her seat, Fern saw that every child had a glass of milk in front of them. When the glasses were drained, Fern noticed a white filmy, un-milk-like residue that clung to the rims. Empty glasses were immediately refilled. Occasionally a child's head would drop with a snoring thump to the tabletop.

"Don't drink the milk," Fern whispered to Francesca. "I think they're putting something in it to make you all sleepy."

Fern turned to pour her milk into a nearby potted plant, but thought back to the Willow, and its scar. She must already have a rotten reputation in the plant world, and didn't want to make it any worse, especially when she needed their help. Francesca watched Fern pour the milk out the barely open window. Beneath the window, two tabby kittens lay hiding from the foul weather. They were delighted by this unexpected gift. They lapped it up like happy children.

"I am looking quite forward to our appointment tomorrow." Dr. Marita Von Svenson appeared at Fern's side. "I love a good session of hypnotherapy. There's nothing I can't find out." The doctor glanced out the window and saw two wet kittens snoring loudly on her lawn.

"Mr. Carruthers!" she barked. "There are kittens littering my lawn!" Francesca quickly poured her own milk out the window. It formed a momentary puddle beneath the window before it dissipated in the deluge.

"Maybe you'll feel better now," Fern said. Francesca smiled.

The children filed into their rooms for the night. Doors were slammed shut. Lights were turned out. Thunder roared, and lightning spliced through the black night. Through the window Fern saw guards patrolling the grounds of the institute. She changed into her hiking clothes. She hadn't counted on this awful storm, or on NITPIC being so well guarded. How on earth was she going to get out of here? Almost instantly her question was answered. An alarm shrieked through the building.

"Flooding! Flooding!" a voice bellowed through the halls. Outside she heard one guard tell another that a large tree branch had crashed through the kitchen roof. Everyone raced toward that wing of NITPIC, their heavy boots thumping through the hallways. Emergency workers were called in from Nedlaw. The tall trees that lined the drive leaned in the wind. Then, the most peculiar thing happened. Fern heard a sound like a scream, or a war whoop, coming from one of the Douglas fir trees. Suddenly, a branch spiraled away from the tree. It spun around and around in the air like a boomerang and struck the power line. Sparks flew as the severed line flopped on the ground like an electric fish. The entire compound went black. Through the dark and wet night, Fern heard words reaching out to her.

"Hurry up! Hurry up! Get out of there! What do you need, an engraved invitation?"

Fern stared out at the trees. They were beckoning to her.

She jammed her belongings into her backpack, grabbed a piece of paper from the desk in her room, and scribbled a note on it. She shoved it into an envelope and addressed it to Olivier Verdant. Fern snuck out into the darkened hall. She could hear the wailing of frightened children. Moving through the corridor, with no guards to stop her, she opened all the doors to the children's rooms. At first hesitant, then eager, the children poured out into the hallway, stumbling every which way. It was easy to get lost in the chaos. Fern inched into Dr. Marita Von Svenson's office, found a stamp in Beatrice Minx's desk and slid her envelope deep into a pile of outgoing mail.

Fern grabbed a rain slicker by the back door, then bolted into the howling night, running down the driveway as fast as she could. Behind her, flashlights flickered in the windows of the institute. From one end of the dark building, children spilled out onto the lawns in their nightclothes. They were soggy little zombies, wandering aimlessly across the soaking grounds. A couple of the children played and splashed in the rain, as though the water were waking them up from a long nap.

Fern knew it was too far to run all the way to town. She went to one of the emergency trucks parked in the driveway and clambered into the back. Pulling a blanket over her head, she waited. *Someone's going to drive to town,* she thought, and eventually, someone did. The driver came out of NITPIC, sprinting through the downpour. As he jumped into the cab, a shout rang out behind him, "More tarps!"

Fern peeked out from her hiding place and watched the NITPIC staff wade through the muck, chasing down their wards. In the distance, a girl with very short orange hair raced through the rain toward the forest behind the institute.

As the truck passed the tall Douglas firs, Fern whispered, "Thank you." She saw Dr. Marita Von Svenson appear at the door of the institute and look out at the mess of children trampling all over her newly landscaped, drenched NITPIC property. Fern hoped she would never have to lay eyes on that awful place or that awful woman again.

In the black of night the truck pulled into the drive of the Nedlaw Hardware Mart, reopened for emergency services. Fern climbed out and ran. She ran through the streets of Nedlaw, darting in and out of the shadows. She ran across the flooded football fields of Joan Baez Middle School and all the way to the Nedlaw train station. On the posted train schedule she saw that a freight train heading south toward Dimple-by-the-Sea would pass through just after midnight.

Fern shivered in the thick bushes by the side of the tracks, waiting for the train. She thought of her father, at home alone. Should she telephone him? He would surely try to stop her. He wouldn't believe Lily was alive. He might even send the police after her. He couldn't help it; after all, he was a parent. Besides, he'd get the letter in a few days, and it would tell him everything he needed to know.

Somewhere in the distance a train engine slowed, preparing for its approach to Nedlaw. The town clock struck midnight. Fern dashed toward the tracks. The train steadily approached the station. A ladder ran down the side of one of the carriages, and she sprinted for it, her boots sliding on the wet grass. Never in a million years would Fern have pictured herself climbing up the rungs of a ladder on a moving train and vaulting into a freight car full of hay, but then people are known to do amazing things in the face of danger.

Fern settled on some hay in the deepest corner of the freight car and pulled the atlas out of her backpack. In the flickering light Fern looked at Dimple-by-the-Sea. It clung to the coast, like Nedlaw, just farther south. According to the schedule, it was a three-hour train ride. Fern was very tired. She hadn't really slept for two days. Up to this moment Fern hadn't given a great deal of thought to the details of her journey. She did now, as she lay against hay bales in a damp and musty freight car, in the middle of the night, with mice—at least that's what she hoped they were—rustling about the corners of the car. Occasional shafts of moonlight flitted through the open doors above the quickly moving trees. She was very much alone. The train car clicked over the rails at a steady pace. Click-click, click-click, click-click, click-click, click-click. It was like a lullaby. Fern's eyes drooped until she couldn't keep them open, and finally she sank into a deep, deep sleep.

Back at NITPIC Dr. Marita Von Svenson was not in a good mood. Her lawn was a mess, and a hundred drugged children had to be herded in from the NITPIC grounds. It took the staff several hours to bring all the muddy children in. Everyone had to shower, and they were all given fresh clothes. Each child was fed more hot milk, and then they were dispatched to their rooms, where they would sleep until at least noon the next day.

NITPIC security guards performed a room check and discovered that Fern Verdant was missing. They immediately reported this to Von Svenson, who seemed strangely calm about it. Later on, a guard arrived at Von Svenson's door to report that Francesca Williams was also missing. No clues as to the disappearances were found. The rain had washed away any telltale footprints.

The next morning Olivier Verdant called NITPIC. He was worried about the ferocious storm that had blown through Nedlaw, and wanted to make sure Fern was all right. Dr. Marita Von Svenson spoke to Olivier in a very soothing and calm voice.

"She's fine."

"Can I speak to her?" Olivier asked.

"I don't think that's wise. You see, we had our first session yesterday. It was very textbook. Fern blames you for her mother's death. She thinks you should have taken better care of your wife." Dr. Marita Von Svenson was very impressed with her own genius. Olivier gasped. "Don't worry, I'll cure her," the doctor added. "Right now, though, I think speaking to her would set her back." Olivier was horrified, but he was a botanist, not a psychiatrist. He felt he had no choice but to trust this expert in the field of childhood insanity.

After the deluge, NITPIC was a mess. Water dripped into hundreds of buckets along the corridors. Von Svenson's assistant, Beatrice Minx, wasn't herself either. Besides the trauma of the storm, her boyfriend, Lucky, had broken up with her that morning over breakfast at the Nedlaw Toast and Roast café. Beatrice spent a good part of her day crying in closets and in the

NITPIC shrubbery. Dr. Marita Von Svenson told Beatrice that she should quit with the "waterworks," that there was enough flooding without Beatrice adding to it.

Beatrice's normal routine was to drop the NITPIC mail at the Nedlaw post office every day. The day after Fern's escape, Beatrice picked up the outgoing mail. In the pile was Fern's hastily scribbled letter to her father. Beatrice shoved the bundle into her satchel. On her way home Beatrice was crying so hard over Lucky that she could barely see the road. She swerved to avoid hitting an emu that had escaped from the nearby Nedlaw Emu Farm. Instead she hit a tree. A passing motorist took her to the hospital, where she was diagnosed with a concussion and kept for observation. Fern's letter to Olivier sat in Beatrice's satchel in her hospital room for three days.

The day after the storm Dr. Marita Von Svenson dialed a long number . . . the kind of number that meant you were trying to reach someone very far away. She waited as the phone rang and rang. Finally someone on the other end of the line picked up.

"Hello, Mr. Saagwalla. You were right. It went exactly as we thought it would." Dr. Marita Von Svenson came very close to smiling.

Lost

Fern woke up to daylight. She had slept so long that an imprint of hay was deeply embedded in her cheek and her arms. She pried herself off the bale, her face looking like an odd fossil. It took her a minute to remember where she was, and why she was there. The train lurched and stopped. Light streaked through the cracks in the boxcar. A terrible thought crept into Fern's mind. According to the train schedule, the ride from Nedlaw to Dimple-by-the-Sea was only supposed to be three hours. She should have arrived at three-thirty in the morning. When it was dark. Not light. Like it was now. Fern sat upright, squinting at the brightness. Then she heard noises. Big, heavy boots shuffling through the train car. She scrunched down into the darkest corner of the compartment. Inching back, she heard a little squeal and saw a mouse back away from her.

"Set some more traps," a big burly voice called out from somewhere. The mouse stopped in its tracks, looked up at Fern as if to say, "Now see what you've done," then hurtled itself through a hole in the floor and fled across the tracks beneath the train. Fern had to get out of here. She would not allow herself to get caught and sent back to her father or, even worse, to NITPIC, where she'd have to submit to Von Svenson's hypnotherapy. The footsteps came closer. The men were unloading the hay. As the bales were thrown through the open door of the freight car, the pile protecting Fern was shrinking and shrinking. Soon there were only six bales hiding her. She was in the midst of inventing a story about being the youngest traveling hay inspector in hay inspector history, when a whistle sounded.

"Break time," a voice boomed from outside. Instantly the boots stopped shuffling and thudded from the car onto the platform. Fern listened. Silence. She peeked through the open door of the car. The backs of two hulking men faced her. Their giant bottoms sank heavily onto the unloaded hay bales. Their heads tipped back as they drank from thermoses. Fern slid out through the opening, dropping to the ground. Their heads bobbed as they chewed their food. Fern pulled her backpack out after her, and it tumbled to the ground. One of the men turned around, but he saw nothing. Fern lay on the ground under the train, behind its great wheels. When the men resumed eating, she crawled along the tracks until they were three cars away from her.

Fern stepped onto the platform, straw sticking out all over her. Above her was a sign. It read *Welcome to the Town of Mystery*.

Mystery? Fern stared at the sign in disbelief. She pulled out her atlas. There it was! Mystery! The town was at least three hundred miles from Dimple-by-the-Sea. She had slept right past her destination! Fern looked around. Aside from the workers there were only two people on the platform. A tall policeman stood leaning against the ticket counter, talking to someone inside. An elderly woman sat on a bench, sketching the stopped freight train. From the looks of the station, this was a tiny town. The woman looked up from her drawing and saw Fern.

"Are you all right, young lady?" she asked.

Fern nodded, unwilling to get into a conversation with a strange adult. The fewer grown-ups she spoke to, the better.

"Where are your parents, dear?" asked the woman.

"They're . . . they're at Dimple-by-the-Sea," Fern answered.

"Oh, well, that's quite a way from here."

"I've got to get there or they'll be worried. My grandmamma put me on the train, and I slept through my stop," Fern fibbed, affecting a lost and innocent expression to further sell her story.

"The next passenger train isn't due until tomorrow morning," the lady added. Then she leaned in very close to Fern's face.

"In fact, I don't believe there has been one since very, very early *this* morning. How exactly did you get here? Why are you covered in hay? It's illegal to steal a ride. Perhaps the nice policeman can help you."

Fern wanted no part of the nice policeman. "You're so kind. Perhaps the nice policeman could help me, but first, I really need to use the bathroom." Fern shifted from one foot to the other, as though the need for a bathroom was imperative. The woman pointed inside the building.

"Thank you." Fern hurried into the train station, and then right on out the front door onto the street. As she looked back over her shoulder, she caught the eye of the woman, who stood watching her. Fern smiled, waved a feeble wave, and walked toward the bathrooms. The moment the woman turned away, Fern bolted. She ran as fast as she could through the small main street of Mystery. She ran past Ye Olde Mystery Meat Shoppe, past the General Store and the Mystery Post Office/Mortuary. Mystery was a small town with a population of two hundred and thirty-one. Everyone knew everyone else. People on the sidewalk took note of the fleeing girl. Fern ran through town in about five minutes. Once the houses and the single gas station had fallen by the wayside, she disappeared into a great wall of green, dense forest.

Fern stopped to catch her breath. Trees surrounded her, the tallest trees she had ever seen. They smelled crisp and clean and fresh. Somewhere nearby she heard the sound of the ocean.

I suppose I'll be safe in the woods, she tried to convince herself. The sky overhead was disappearing behind the thick umbrella of branches. Fern heard a noise coming toward her. It was the unmistakable sound of feet falling on leaves, and snapping twigs. She headed deeper into the forest.

"Hey! You! Kid! Come back here!" Fern looked back and saw the blue of the policeman's uniform.

"It's dangerous in these woods!" he shouted after her.

72

Fern ran as fast as her legs would carry her, dodging low-hanging boughs, jumping over fallen limbs. Fern was not particularly fast. She had never been good at gym class, and except for her recent trial for the Baez Bulldogs cheerleading squad she'd spent most of her time reading or on the computer. Fern's main interest was avoiding any interest in botany. Her mother had tried to take her hiking, but Fern whined her way out of it. The only athletic thing she could do was swim. The Verdants had taken her to lessons when she was too young to protest.

"Do you want me to have to fetch the search dogs?" the police officer bellowed after her.

No, she certainly did not, but she wasn't about to give up her freedom. She ploughed on, stumbling and fumbling through the forest, tripping and bruising, cutting and scraping, while the policeman blundered behind her. Fern raced blindly ahead, so blindly that she did not see the pool of slimy green sludge in front of her until she splashed facedown in the stinky slop. It smelled like rotten, dead things—like the disgusting mulch her parents used to fertilize their garden. She could hear the policeman gaining on her, and desperately yanked first one, then the other foot, but the sludge was thick and her feet didn't move. Thick vines crept around her ankles, and quickly wrapped themselves snakelike around her legs. Each time she pulled there was a deep sucking sound followed by a slowly popping bubble of muck on the surface. It felt as though the vines were trying to drag her down into the mire. Her backpack was heavy. She looked over her shoulder and saw the policeman's badge glinting in the shafts of light that pierced the tall treetops.

Panic set in. In her mind she silently screamed, *I've got to get out of here!* Then she felt something strange.

"Agggggghhhhh!" The thing crept beneath her body, inching along her belly.

"Agggggghhhhh!" she screamed again, as whatever it was cradled her, slowly, firmly pulling her out of the muck.

"Shut up, eh!" A strongly accented voice entered her head, as a leafy branch slapped itself over her mouth.

The thing thrashed around, severing the vines that pulled at her ankles. It lifted her above the ground, sweeping her higher and higher into the air. She wiped the swamp water out of her eyes and looked down. The ground receded below. What on earth was happening? She wriggled and a voice said, "Don't squirm or I'll drop ya, eh, you're slimy."

Fern felt branches poking into her. She was being held in the limbs of a giant eucalyptus tree. It carried her swiftly ten, twenty, thirty, forty feet up and away from the earth, and the policeman. Fern let out a muffled scream. The tree flinched, and kept moving. When the tree had completely straightened, she looked down and saw the speck of a policeman, eighty feet beneath her, running through the woods. Beyond the tops of the trees she could see to the ocean.

"G'day," said the Eucalyptus in a very thick Australian accent.

"Hello," Fern answered nervously aloud. She looked down. "I think I'm going to throw up."

"Then don't look down," the Eucalyptus said. "Look out to sea. It's going to be a beautiful sunset. Best time of the day."

"Sunset?" Fern realized the light that had woken her on the train was not morning light, but the light of late afternoon. She had slept through a whole day. No wonder she was so far from her destination. She clung onto a branch.

"Are you Australian?"

"Good guess," answered the Eucalyptus. "My ancestors were Australian. That's where all eucalyptuses came from. Never actually seen the motherland myself, but I feel it in my soul."

Fern looked around; she was in a stand of eucalyptus trees. A hundred trees mumbled in agreement.

"Thanks for helping me. I would never have gotten out of that disgusting mud . . . but how did you know I was there?"

"I heard your thoughts. Bloody deafening they was." Fern realized that in her panic she had inadvertently spoken telepathically with the tree.

"Plus I had me ears and eyes open for you. Everyone does. There was an APB sent out."

"APB?"

"An 'All Plants Bulletin.' Went out last night from a group of firs somewhere up the coast. Message came through the grapevine. Awful lot of gossip on you banging about." Fern realized that the firs lining the NITPIC driveway, the same ones that had helped her escape, must have sent the APB.

"We're all to keep a keen eye out for you. Help if we can. Those that want ta help, that is," added the Eucalyptus.

"I don't understand."

"Yer mum's a hero. Bloody well revered all around the world. Why, my own cousin down Tasmania way worships her.

He was one of the smaller species of eucalyptus, just a shrub really . . . last of his kind. Yer mum swooped in and saved the day. Yup, young Ernest was downright daggy, but yer mum fixed him all up. She's darn near a saint."

"I had no idea . . . ," Fern said.

"Well, no, you wouldn't. I mean, you've only just gotten the gift, or so word has it." The Eucalyptus paused, contemplating the enormity of Fern's gift. "Quite a responsibility. Talk about weight of the world. Glad it's not me."

"Thanks a lot." Fern had only one thought about her gift, and that was how it could help her find her mother. She hadn't really spent any time thinking about her far-reaching responsibilities. It was annoying that a whole world of plants knew quite a bit about her, while she knew nothing about them.

"I have to get to Dimple-by-the-Sea, that's the only thought on my mind at the moment."

"Well, actually, mate, you don't," replied the Eucalyptus.

"Of course I do. You don't understand."

" 'Fraid I do, mate. You've become something of a celebrity in our world. Since you told that Willow with the giant cake-hole yer plans, she's been yammering and yammering about it. It's caused a bit of a divide. Yer mum's message said that you shouldn't look for her, that it was too risky. Some of the plants in the plant world feel they'd be betraying her wishes if they helped you. They say that if something happened to you, then we'd all be up a creek without a paddle. The last protector would be gone. That Fir tree in Dimple-by-the-Sea is one of them types. He worships yer mum. Won't tell you nuthin'. Then there are those of us who don't want to see yer mum . . . um . . . never come back . . . that want to help you rescue her. If it hadn't been for yer mum . . . who knows what would have happened to young Ernest." The Eucalyptus sounded like he was fighting back tears.

"Some of us have also lost someone near and dear. We understand how you feel. So, some in our world wish to help, and others don't. Then there's those few that um . . . how shall I put it . . . don't wish the best for you at all."

Fern barely heard this last comment. "How can I find my mother if the Fir won't speak to me?"

"We'll have to give a think on that," said the Eucalyptus.

The sun was hovering on the horizon. Fern noticed a fishing boat bobbing in the calm waters just off shore. It was bright orange with a rainbow-colored porpoise painted on the side. Underneath the colorful creature were the words *The Porpoise*. Slashes of red sunset reflected on the boat. The combination of red and orange made the boat appear to be on fire. It was beautiful.

"Ya must be bushwhacked."

Fern's attention drifted away from the vessel. "I am." Fern guessed that bushwhacked meant "tired."

"Stay up here for the night. I'll keep an eye out for you. There are all kinds of creepers and crawlers on the forest floor after dark."

"I've never slept in a tree before."

"I guess there are many things you've never done before that you'll be doing now," answered the Eucalyptus.

The tree was right. Her life had changed. It would never be as simple as it once was, even though she hadn't thought that it *was* very simple at all. Fern stared at the moon, wondering how she'd find her mother, and thinking as many thoughts as there were stars in the night sky.

"I don't mean to be rude, but what is it like to be a tree? Don't you get awfully bored being in the same place all the time with nothing to do?"

"Not likely. In fact . . . never. Nature is a wonderful thing, aye. Every single day is different from the last. Ya can't beat fresh air and sunshine and birds nesting in your limbs. Besides, I wouldn't trade one single sunrise for life as one of you. The people I've seen never appear to be content. That's their problem. Always busy doing something . . . planning something . . . never just *being*."

Fern lay in the branches, thinking how odd life without television or a computer would be, and finally dozed off. The next morning when she opened her eyes she found a pile of fruits and nuts lying on a nearby branch. There were apples, pears, and walnuts. As she hungrily bit into an apple, she had a shocking thought.

"Wait! If I can talk with you . . . then can I talk to an apple too?" Fern spat out the bite, horrified.

"That's like me asking if I could have a conversation with your hair," the Eucalyptus laughed.

Their chat was interrupted by the sound of barking dogs. A

stream of police plowed through the forest, being led by blood-hounds, their noses sniffing along the ground.

"Duck," cried one of the officers. "I've been hit . . . we're under attack!" A chunk of chewed apple bounced off his shoulder. The policemen all fell to the ground, drawing their guns, but there was no sound except for the wind rustling through the eucalyptus trees. The officer looked about and found a bite of apple with teeth marks on it.

"False alarm," he held out the apple piece, "but this isn't an apple tree." All the policemen looked up. The bloodhounds looked up and barked wildly, scratching at the base of the tree. The Eucalyptus winced as their claws tore his bark. Fern ducked into the branches.

"It's an eighty-foot-tall tree. How's a kid, especially a girl, going to climb that?" said a particularly oafish-looking police-man. Fern was insulted. Even if she *hadn't* climbed the tree, how dare he presume she couldn't! The oaf kicked the dogs for mak-ing a mistake. The dogs were upset by this abuse. They knew they were right, but the fools in the blue uniforms following them didn't trust them. The disgusted dogs agreed among them-selves to intentionally lead their masters astray, just to get even.

"She probably spit it out while she was running," said an-other policeman. The dogs looked at each other as if to say "What an idiot!", and took off in the wrong direction.

Fern watched all of this silently. When the dogs and the men had moved on, she hungrily devoured the rest of the apple, and then started eating a pear. She hadn't realized how starving she was.

"I have an idea," Fern said, in between bites. Sometimes an idea will come to you in the middle of the night while you're fast asleep. This had happened to Fern.

"An idea?" responded the Eucalyptus.

"Yes. You said that you'd help me, and that there were a lot of other plants and trees out there that might want to help me."

"Yes," the Eucalyptus said, a little cautiously.

"Well, I want to send out an All Plants Bulletin asking plants who wish to cooperate to come forward with any information they may have that will help me find my mother. I need *you* to send it out. I can barely send one thought to one plant, let alone a complicated thought to an entire world of plants."

"Don't be a mug!" said the Eucalyptus. "If I did that, all kinds of plants would be notified, including the bad ones, the ones who would want to do you harm."

"Why would any plant want to do me harm?"

"There are some twining, whinging, strangling plants that will always survive, like cockroaches. They'll never need your help, and would happily take over any vacant plot of soil. They don't care which plants die. As far as they're concerned, if you and ya mum were out of the way, there would be more species croaking, and more room for them. Trust me, those creeps will never help you . . . in fact, quite the opposite. Didn't you feel them pulling at you from the bottom of the swamp?"

"It doesn't matter. I have to take that risk. If that tree in Dimple-by-the-Sea is too 'honorable' and won't help me, then I have to find others who will." Fern looked off into the distance and noticed that the orange fishing boat she'd seen the previous evening was gone. "Now," she turned her attention back to the Eucalyptus, "would you please send out the APB?"

The Eucalyptus was quiet.

"Please?"

"All right . . . all right!" the Eucalyptus said.

"Good. This is what I want you to say." Fern took a note she'd written out of her knapsack. She cleared her throat and read.

" 'Attention, plants of the world! This is Fern Verdant. I am the daughter of Lily Verdant, protector of plants. My mother is in terrible danger, and I have to find her. If you have any information that might help me do that, please contact me as soon as possible. It's a matter of life and death!' "

"Use your noggin!" The Eucalyptus was horrified. "You don't know what you might be in for here. It's like telling the bad ones, 'Here I am, come and get me!' "

"Do you have a better plan?" asked Fern. The Eucalyptus did not.

"Are you sure?" it asked.

Fern nodded.

"Well then, hold on to your knickers!" And with that the Eucalyptus sent out the message as far and wide as it possibly could. Fern sat back in the branches to wait. She was nervous. She was well aware that whatever good news might come, there might also be bad.

The Plot

It had been a month since Lily sent her message through the plant world to Fern. That's how long it had taken for the message to make its way to her daughter. Even though she was unconscious, Lily was worried about Fern. She had heard rumblings and mumblings through the Silver Rose. She knew about an extremely gossipy weeping willow in Nedlaw. She knew about NITPIC. And she knew that Fern was looking for her. This was the last thing Lily wanted. If there was some way to let Olivier know his daughter was headed for danger, she would have told him, but Lily could only communicate with plants, and plants could only communicate with those who had the gift.

Lily and the Silver Rose remained in the cave in Sri Lanka, halfway around the world from Nedlaw. Shaped like a teardrop, Sri Lanka is full of beautiful caves decorated with golden statues of the Buddha. Lily was not in one of those caves. She was in a plain, dank, dark one. Claude Hubris was trying desperately to wake her up. He attached electrodes to her head and sent electricity through her body to jolt her back to consciousness. For amusement, Luella let her python slither over Lily. Luella was getting very bored with this situation.

"Who does he think he is, keeping us waiting like this?" Luella complained. Claude looked at his wife in disbelief.

"*We* know who he is, and he'll get here when he gets here."

Luella shut up. Actually she wished Saagwalla would never arrive.

"He's not exactly pleased she's in a coma," Claude reminded her. The couple tried not to imagine the punishment Saagwalla would inflict upon them.

Each night Claude and Luella drove to Henry Saagwalla's palatial cliff-top hideout, leaving the mossy-haired Chia Man to guard their prisoner. When spiders skittered over Lily, crawling up her arms and legs, the Chia Man would brush them off.

One quiet, damp evening Lily was lying silently, as usual, when the strangest thing happened. She heard an unfamiliar voice whisper the words "Poor thing" into her mind. Where on earth had this voice come from? Except for the Silver Rose, there were no other plants in this deep, dark cave—nothing could survive in here. Only one other creature inhabited the cave, the Chia Man.

"Who's there?" Lily asked telepathically. There was only silence.

"Who could it be?" the Rose asked Lily.

"What about . . . ?" Lily directed her thoughts toward the Chia Man. "Was it you?" The Chia Man quickly receded into the dimness of the cave.

The next morning Claude and Luella came to the cave earlier than usual. Luella's hair was piled absurdly on her head and held in place by several geckos. She wore a baby leopard shawl draped across her shoulders. Luella and Claude seemed very jittery. The air was electric with their anxiety.

"Do something!" Luella shrieked. "Wake her up!"

"How do you propose I do that?" asked Claude.

"What about one of Saagwalla's potions? Did you check the laboratory?"

Claude looked at his wife, supremely irritated.

"Don't you think that's the first thing I tried to do?" Claude answered. "It's locked up as tight as a drum."

They both stared glumly at the woman in a coma, pondering their fate. Things weren't going as they'd planned.

"Maybe we should just leave—run away," said Luella. Claude was considering this option when a deep, rumbling sound grumbled from the earth. The whole cave vibrated. Luella clung to Claude's lapels. A crack appeared in the floor of the cave, a six-foot-long slit separating the Hubrises from Lily. They stared at it in horror.

"What's happening?" Luella whimpered.

"I haven't got the faintest idea?" answered a very nervous Claude.

Lily and the Silver Rose were just as mystified as the Hubrises. The gap in the floor widened. The Silver Rose described the spectacle to Lily. On closer inspection, the rock floor of the cave was only a thin surface, maybe half an inch thick, covering a set of steel doors that slid apart. Below the doors, the top step of a staircase revealed itself, leading down into darkness. The smell of an even danker, even deeper subterranean cavern wafted up to the Hubrises. Out of this black void stepped Henry Saagwalla.

Luella Hubris screamed. She was never prepared for the awfulness of Saagwalla's face even though they'd worked for him for some time now. Weren't scars supposed to heal with time? She didn't understand that the poison in Saagwalla's heart had deepened his disfigurement. Frightened, Luella's leopard wrap yowled and leapt off her shoulders, slinking out the door with its ears pinned back in fear. The geckos sprang from her head, and her hair fell in front of her face. Henry Saagwalla smiled. He loved the effect he had on people.

"Surprise!" said Saagwalla in a deep voice. He looked at the comatose botanist. His expression turned bleak.

"I see there has been no progress."

Saagwalla snapped his fingers, and a man appeared on the stairs behind him. This was Leslie, Saagwalla's most trusted sidekick.

Leslie was a short, muscular albino with an expertise in martial arts. He was of indeterminate age; he could have been twenty, he could have been fifty. His skin was as white as chalk. His hair stood up on end. Leslie stared at the Hubrises expressionless. Luella and Claude waited for the worst.

"I—I—I'm sure she'll wake up soon," dithered Claude. "It was an accident . . . couldn't be helped."

Saagwalla stepped over to Lily's gurney. He looked down at the unconscious and beautiful botanist. "You don't think I'd trust the two of you with my entire plan, do you?" He picked up a lock of Lily's hair. "Quite a sleeping beauty—isn't she?"

The equipment monitoring Lily's vital signs started pinging, gauges started swinging, and the machine that kept track of Lily's heartbeat went haywire. A shudder went through Lily's body as though a snake had rippled through her veins.

"Excellent," Saagwalla said. "She knows I am here." As the words came out of his mouth, the lock of Lily's hair in his hand turned silver-gray.

Too Much Information

Fern had no idea what to expect after the Eucalyptus sent out the All Plants Bulletin. At first the messages dribbled in slowly.

"Poor girl misses her mother," murmured one plant.

"What are you doing messing with APBs?" demanded another.

"Don't pursue this!" warned the third.

After the initial dribs and drabs, the messages came in fast and furious, like pages swept briskly along by a sudden gust of wind. Ten, twenty, thirty, and more and more and more.

"Bad girl!"

"Good girl!"

"Disrespectful girl!"

"Loving girl!"

"Go away!"

"Quick, you must find her!"

"Good luck!"

"Drop dead!"

Fern didn't know how many messages were collecting in her head. Everyone had an opinion, and each message competed for her attention. Some plants cursed her, others said that even if they had information, they couldn't send it; after all, Lily Verdant did not want her daughter put in harm's way, and they were very loyal to Lily.

It was as if thousands of Post-it Notes had flown through the air and stuck themselves onto Fern's head. She felt like a bulletin board. The notes streamed into her brain with such force that she nearly fell out of the tree. How on earth was she going to get through them all?

"Can you help me with some of these?" she asked the Eucalyptus.

"Sorry, mate," responded the tree, "they're addressed to you. You can't go around mucking about with someone else's messages. Downright illegal, that is."

Fern sifted through them one at a time. It was tedious. Some potted plants with no information at all begged to come along as sidekicks, just to get out of their rut. Other, older vegetation chided her for being headstrong, for not paying any attention to her mother's wishes. A couple of saplings relayed their yearning for the open road and no responsibilities.

Some creeping vines said they'd accompany her on any journey anywhere, but the Eucalyptus explained they were the same plants that opposed Lily's work and had tried to pull Fern under in the swamp. On and on and on it went. Hours went by. It was past noon, and very hot. The Eucalyptus fanned her. By now Fern had been in the same muddy clothes for two days. She was quite stinky, and had remnants of swamp stuck to her. Her long black curls were tangled and bits of muck poked out of her hair. It was as if she'd been in the forest for weeks.

"You might consider getting a bath at some point," said the Eucalyptus in a voice that sounded like he was pinching his nose, wherever that was. "There's a waterfall not far from here." Fern wasn't really listening. Determined, she pored through the messages one by one, until finally, something caught her attention.

"Listen to this!" Fern jumped up excitedly, forgetting she was eighty feet in the air. She wobbled wildly when she looked down, then sat back in the fork of two branches and read.

" 'Dear Miss Verdant, I received your query earlier, and must tell you that I helped pass your mother's message along to you. I received it during the last full moon and relayed it up the coast, as instructed, north toward Nedlaw. A Fir tree in Dimple-by-the-Sea picked it up. The thing is, I don't know whom the message came from because I'd never heard a plant like it before. It wasn't like a regular plant. It sounded grating and harsh; more like a machine than a plant. It hurt to receive it. I'm sorry I can't be of more help. Wishing you the best of luck, from a Cherry Tree residing in Crescent City.' "

"What does it mean . . . a machine? Can plants communicate with mechanical things?"

"Not likely," said the Eucalyptus. "Stuff it if I'm not

stymied." Fern pulled out her atlas and located Crescent City on the map. It was about a hundred miles north of Mystery. She traced the course of the message. It had traveled from the south, up the west coast to Nedlaw. But where had it originated? In Mexico or Panama or maybe even Chile?

Fern was exhausted and filthy. Taking the Eucalyptus's advice, she decided to get a bath. Maybe it would refresh her, help her think more clearly. The Eucalyptus refused to let Fern walk to the waterfall.

"Some of those creepers are still down there, praying you'll drop in on them, and you never know when those dogs are likely to return." The Eucalyptus had a chat with the other trees in the vicinity, and they agreed to take her to the falls. This was how Fern found herself being passed along from treetop to treetop, eighty feet above the ground. She could hear the trees talking to each other.

"Phew, she stinks."

"Good God, you'd think someone would have told her."

"Shhhh, that's what mothers do and you know her mother isn't . . ."

"Shut up. She can hear us."

Eventually Fern was floating above a rocky opening. The trees gently lowered her down, bough by bough, until she found herself near a small waterfall that flowed into a crystal clear pond. She hung her backpack on a branch and jumped into the pool with all her clothes on. The water was crisp and cool. It felt good to wash off the last two days. She scrubbed her face and plunged under the water. Resurfacing, she floated on her back, looking up at the sun as it filtered through the leafy canopy above her. There were a couple of lily pads off in a corner of the pond. They were gently humming to themselves. The music was calming. By the side of the pond a small grove of ferns unfurled.

"We'll keep an eye out for you," they said. They looked like lacy emerald umbrellas. The irony of this was not lost on Fern; the very plants she despised were looking out for her.

"Thank you," Fern said, choking on a little gulp of pond water. This, she thought, would be another advantage to communicating with plants telepathically . . . she'd be able to keep her mouth shut while chatting in ponds. In the distance the low buzz of plant conversation comforted her. Fern always thought it must have been very lonely for her mother, traipsing around the world without her family. Now, she realized that her mother had friends everywhere. She dipped below the surface of the water again, the tendrils of her jet-black hair floating about her. She drifted back up, eyes blinking into the sunlight.

"Frezzzzssnndd meesszzz!!!!!!!!!!!!!!!" Out of nowhere the sound seared into Fern's head like a branding iron. It was a mind-piercing shriek that shattered the silence with such intensity that she clasped her hands to her ears and sank below the surface of the pond.

"Frezzzzssnndd meesszzz!!!!!!!!!!!!!" scraped through her skull again. The words, if you could even call them words, erupted in bursts, as if it were difficult for the speaker to speak them. It sounded like metal scraping on metal. Fern swam to the surface of the pond. Her head hurt.

"Frezzzzssnndd meesszzz," it repeated. "Frend meez," then, "Fend mez . . . Fend mez," over and over and over, until Fern's head ached. "Fern Verdant!!! Find me!"

"Who are you?" Fern called out, her head throbbing. One final word bit into her head.

"Explosions!"

Fern splashed out of the water and collapsed to the ground, holding her head. She staggered to her backpack and called out to the nearest tree.

"Please! Take me back to the Eucalyptus, now!" One of the trees swooped down and picked her up. By the time she got back to the Eucalyptus, she was very weak. The Eucalyptus cradled her in its branches.

"I received a message so painful I thought my head was going to explode," Fern told him, afraid the pain might return. "I think it was from the 'thing' that the Cherry Tree mentioned. It didn't feel like a plant. It wanted help. It said the word *explosions*." The Eucalyptus was puzzled.

"There, there," it said, "have a rest."

Fern lay in the branches of the tree, gazing out over the horizon. Far in the distance she saw the rolling glow of a lighthouse. Pulling her atlas out of her bag, she flipped to the page highlighting Oregon. No such town as "Explosion." She stared up into the blackness, thinking. Finally, cradled in eucalyptus branches, she fell asleep.

The next morning Fern packed up her backpack. "I have to leave," she told the Eucalyptus.

"Hey, mate, ya can't go now, you don't know where you're going."

"Maybe not exactly, but all of these messages keep coming from the south. I can at least start out in that direction."

"What about the bloodhounds? What if they come back?"

"Perhaps you could arrange for the trees to pass me along to the ocean. Then I could walk along the water's edge, and wouldn't leave a trace."

"I don't think it's safe."

"I'm not going to sit here and wait. The longer my mom's a prisoner, the more likely something bad could happen to her." The Eucalyptus couldn't argue with that. A short while later Fern bid farewell to the helpful tree.

"I'll be sure to let you know how everything turns out. Thank you for your kindness and all your help." Fern hugged a branch goodbye.

"Be careful!" the Eucalyptus's voice was full of concern. "Don't take any unnecessary chances." It surrounded her with its fragrant leaves then reluctantly passed her along to the next tree, which complained about the weight of her backpack. The Eucalyptus had packed a supply of fruits and nuts for her journey. Fern was passed from treetop to treetop. At the edge of the woods she was gingerly set down atop a cliff overlooking the sea.

The cliffs gave way to a sandy shoreline that stretched ahead as far as she could see. Fern took off her hiking boots and put them in her backpack. She stepped into the cool water. The surf washed across her feet, and she started her journey southward. She walked for miles. The sun was pleasant and warm, not too hot yet. Fern kept walking, not knowing where she'd sleep or how long it would take to find answers to her questions.

The coastline was remote. No one played on the beaches or swam in the sea. One little cove led to another. Fern walked and walked. She stopped for lunch in the shade of the cliff. She drank some of her water and ate an apple. Pulling out her atlas, she looked to see what the next town south of Mystery was. The map was blank for many miles. Perhaps there was some tiny hamlet too small to make it onto a map. She packed up her things and continued on.

Afternoon inched into late afternoon. Rounding a rocky promontory, Fern was startled by the chatter of voices. Ahead of her was a sandy bay. Kids screamed happily and played in the surf. Sandcastles stood on the beach. Parents called after children in the water. Behind them a sign announced *Dollop Public Beach*. The beach was edged with tall brown grasses, which gave way to a road that cut through the trees, leading to, Fern presumed, Dollop. A small cluster of beach shacks selling chowder and corn on the cob lined the edge of the sand.

There was an old lifeguard station on the beach, and in it sat an old lifeguard. He was watching the children in the surf. An ice cream truck played a tinkling bell version of "Itsy Bitsy Spider." The notes wafted through the lazy afternoon heat. South of the beach was the lighthouse Fern had spied from the top of the Eucalyptus tree. Fern was hungry for something other than fruit, nuts, and energy bars. She made a beeline for the snack shacks. She didn't know what to order first, so she ordered one of everything, paying for it with some of her savings.

Fern parked herself on a sun-bleached log that separated the sand from the parking lot and the concession stands. She hungrily finished an ice cream waffle, a bowl of corn chowder, and an order of French fries in record time. She watched the happy families building sandcastles and playing in the surf. Would her own family ever be that way again? But her own family had never been like that, and probably never would be. She missed them anyway. Fern was startled from her thoughts by a voice.

"Miss?" Fern looked up to find the lifeguard towering above her. He was at least fifty years old, and he didn't look too happy about being a lifeguard. His paunchy stomach hung out over a tiny red Speedo swimsuit, which was not flattering. A gold hoop earring made him look like a portly pirate. His baseball hat announced his name, Big Dog. He had a tattoo on the remnant of an arm muscle, which read *Pain in the Butt*. He leaned over Fern, his bulk casting a huge shadow.

"Where are your parents?" Big Dog asked. Fern did not want to be identified as a runaway. She pointed up behind her, to the road.

"In Dollop," she said. "We ran out of sunblock." He looked at her through suspicious squinty eyes. She stared right back at him.

"It's not safe to leave children on the beach by themselves."

"I'm not a child. I'm thirteen, and besides, you're here to make sure I'm okay."

"You shouldn't talk back to grown-ups," Big Dog growled, displeased at having this impertinent interloper in his sandy little kingdom. "I'm going to be watching you. If you do one thing wrong, one thing, you're toast! Remember, I'm the king of *this* beach!" He waddled back toward his lifeguard station, his swimsuit wedged up his bottom. As soon as his back was turned, Fern bolted toward the woods edging the beach. She hid among the trees, trying hard not to accidentally communicate with them in case some creepers found her. She watched the fat lifeguard until the sun was setting and the beach was deserted. The shacks closed up. The lifeguard walked toward the woods. He scanned the area, his eyes squinting out of his leathery face, white sunblock on his lips. It was as if he knew she was hiding there. After the sun went down, the lifeguard climbed into his pickup truck and roared out of the dusty parking lot.

Fern made her way to the lifeguard station. She crept inside and lay down on the floor, resting her head on her backpack, trying to ignore all the night noises outside. Eventually the sound of the waves tumbling to shore put her to sleep.

Fern was having all kinds of dreams about her mother, Olivier, NITPIC, creepers, ferns, and Grandmamma Lisette, when she was wakened by a huge bang. She sat up startled, in that dopey way a person does when they're woken from a deep sleep.

It took her a minute to figure out where she was. Peeking outside the hut, she scanned the beach. Nothing. Then, in the moonlight, out in the sea, she saw the same boat she'd seen the other day, the brightly colored *Porpoise*. It was anchored off

96

the lighthouse. Fern heard another loud bang. Above the boat, a mountain of fireworks exploded. Fountains of sunflower yellow and piercing pink melted into the water. Fern sat on the ramp that led up to the lifeguard's hut, watching. The night fell dark and silent again. Another bang erupted in streams of peacock blue, vermillion, emerald, and gold. It was like a rainbow melting into the sea. Fern had never seen such beautiful fireworks. She watched in awe, wondering what wonderful thing the people on the boat were celebrating. Each new burst of color was followed by a moment's darkness, and silence. She stared, riveted, until yet another explosion of color followed.

"Such beautiful fireworks," she said to herself. Fern didn't hear the truck pull into the beach parking lot, but she did notice the headlights illuminating the lifeguard hut. Fern scrambled back inside and shut the door behind her. The headlights flicked off. She hid in the darkness. Her heart beat wildly. As another explosion sounded outside, it dawned on her.

" 'Explosions!' " she whispered to herself. "Those were 'explosions' blasting off the orange boat!" Outside she heard a loud voice.

"This is my beach, Mitzi! I'm the king of the beach." Fern recognized the voice of Big Dog.

"The whole beach, really? Is this whole beach yours?" Mitzi chirped back.

Fern peered out the window of the lifeguard station. Big Dog stood beside the little elevated shack. He was swaying, even though there was no breeze. He wore skintight jeans and an undershirt with the words *Big Dog* written on it. Mitzi stood beside him wearing a brightly colored flowered dress, also swaying. Her blond hair was piled on her head. A spray of pink fireworks shot off the deck of the *Porpoise*. Reflected in the glow, Mitzi's hair looked like a heap of pink cotton candy.

"Aren't they beautiful?" Mitzi said. The lifeguard frowned in the direction of the boat. Then a strange look passed across his eyes. It was an idea.

"I arranged it just for you."

"But we just met tonight," Mitzi looked at him, confused.

Fern rolled her eyes and turned her attention back to the boat. She had a strong feeling that she was supposed to be on it. Scanning the hut she noticed a buoy hanging on the wall, the kind a lifeguard would use to rescue someone. It was long and red with handles on the side and a rope attached to it. It was perfect! Big Dog and Mitzi were clambering up the ramp to the hut door. Fern slid the buoy out the window. It fell onto the sand with a dull thud, but the breaking of the waves masked the sound. She dropped her backpack out after it. Footsteps thudded up the ramp.

"Hey!" yelled the lifeguard. "Where's my buoy? Someone stole my buoy!" He looked at the window just in time to see Fern disappear through it.

"Get back here, you brat! That's Dollop town property you're stealing!" Big Dog yelled, lumbering down the ramp. Fern raced across the sand toward the water's edge, her backpack and the buoy slowing her down. Big Dog's stomach slowed him down even more. He stumbled and tripped after Fern. Mitzi stumbled and tripped after him—it was difficult running in the sand in stiletto heels. The lifeguard closed in on the girl, as Fern flung herself into the ocean, clinging to the buoy and kicking wildly. Big Dog was only a few feet from her, but he pulled up short, teetering at the water's edge. The Pacific Ocean licked his toes.

"Go get her!" shouted Mitzi. "That's your buoy." But Big Dog didn't budge. He didn't put one foot into the water. Mitzi looked at him, puzzled. She didn't know that Big Dog hadn't actually set foot in the water in twenty-one years, and in that time he'd developed a deathly fear of the ocean and all the mysteries that lurked below its surface.

Fern paddled faster and faster toward the *Porpoise*. When she looked over her shoulder, she saw Big Dog stamping his feet in anger at the water's edge.

Anthony

The *Porpoise* was farther out to sea than Fern anticipated. The fireworks had seemed so close to shore, but by now they had subsided and the lights in the boat had been turned off. Occasionally the rotating glow of the lighthouse beam flickered over the boat. It is very dark out in the ocean at night. Fern couldn't see an inch beneath her. The water was cold, much colder than it had been in the daylight. Splashing about on a sunny sandy beach was one thing, but thrashing your way into a pitch-black ocean at night was another. Fern was frightened. Then, in the dark, forbidding night, she heard it again.

"Fern Verdant! Rescue me!" The grating voice was louder, clearer.

It was definitely coming from the *Porpoise*. She focused on the boat bobbing out ahead. Kicking hard, she made steady progress. Fern tried to rein in her imagination—better not wonder what creepy, scaly, giant fish might be just below the surface. She had an icky image of hundreds of fish taking hold of the strands of her hair, and tugging her down to the murky floor of the sea; after all, she was trespassing in their territory. She kicked harder. The more her imagination ran wild, the faster she kicked, and the closer she got to the boat. Maybe being afraid was a good thing. She felt that way right up until a slimy presence brushed up against her leg.

"Agggghhhhh!" Fern's scream was lost amid the sounds of the sea. She kicked harder. Whatever it was brushed against her again. *How many times do sharks circle before they attack?* thought Fern. There it was again . . . and again. No matter how hard she kicked, she wasn't moving. Something had wrapped itself around one leg and was pulling her toward the shore, while something else had wrapped itself around the end of the buoy and was pulling her toward the boat. She was being tugged in two opposite directions, and going nowhere fast. She tried to wriggle away, to no avail.

Fern was afraid to look beneath the surface, but she knew she had to, like those people in horror movies who hear a noise in a dark basement and go down the stairs to investigate. She took a gulp of air and stuck her head under the water. Beneath her she found a bed of languorous seaweed, undulating with the rhythm of the tide.

"What are you doing?" The words bubbled angrily out of Fern's mouth. She surfaced, choking on sea water.

"Lily Verdant doesn't want you hurt!" blurted one bit of seaweed telepathically.

"Lily Verdant must be saved!" blurted out another bit of seaweed. Fern was being held hostage by a patch of squabbling seaweed.

"This is ridiculous!" Fern gurgled. "I'm not moving anywhere, and it's freezing." Fern was getting colder and colder. She gasped for air and kicked, but it was no use, she wasn't budging an inch. The seaweed held firm. Fern clung onto the buoy.

"Let me go!" Fern was becoming dizzy. "You're going to drown me! I've already been in the water too long, if you don't help me get to that boat"—Fern bobbed in the chilly waves like a human cork—"someone will have to inform my mother that you two were responsible for my death!" Suddenly, her legs were freed. The boat was still quite far off. She kicked sluggishly toward it, but being cold had taken its toll and she seemed to make no progress at all. The waves had grown stronger, pushing her back toward the shore. She was paddling in place and exhausted.

"I can't make it," Fern cried out. The seaweed was horrified. Fern heard some squabbling from underneath her. Neither faction wanted to be deemed responsible for the death of a protector. In an instant Fern was suddenly moving quickly through the water, racing toward the boat, faster than her kicks could have ever carried her. She skimmed the surface, practically surfing. The seaweed had joined forces to pass her along, as if she were in a giant mosh pit. In no time at all Fern found herself face to face with the words *The Porpoise*. The seaweed disappeared below her into the inky water, apologizing profusely. A ladder led up the side of the boat. Fern struggled up the rungs and onto the deck.

As Fern set foot on the deck, a loud "Noooooooooo!" screeched into her head. In an instant, she found herself enveloped in a giant black fishing net and suspended upside down in the air, like a flounder on the end of a line. Fern bobbed in the net in the cool night. The lights in the cabin flashed on. Panicked whispers sounded from below. Jutting out from the corner of the deck, Fern saw the deadly metal of a harpoon pointed right at her. Holding the harpoon was a slender blond boy. He was about fourteen, and had the golden complexion of someone who spent much of his time in the sun. His eyes were glued on the soggy body dripping from the net above him. Hesitantly, four others emerged from below deck; two more boys and two girls, all eyes trained on Fern.

"Shoot it!" yelled a smaller boy, maybe eight years old, with a long scar cutting through the perfect skin of his face.

"Be quiet, Kai," said the harpoon-carrying boy, who seemed to be the eldest, and the leader. Kai looked down, embarrassed at being chastised in front of the group.

"Who are you?" asked the leader. "What are you doing here?"

Fern didn't answer. She didn't know what to answer.

"I said . . . who are you? Don't you speak English?"

Silence. The boy was getting irritated, and waved the

harpoon around erratically. Fern figured she'd better say something.

"I'm lost," called Fern down to the group. At that moment the dim glow of the lighthouse beacon passed across them and the leader realized for the first time that his captive was no older than he was. The boy stared at her . . . then lowered his harpoon.

"Let her down, she's just a kid."

Fern was insulted. She certainly didn't feel like "just a kid" after everything she'd been through. The net lurched to the ground and Fern landed on her bottom. Kai and the others peeled back the mesh, while the leader trained the harpoon at Fern's heart.

"Who are you?" he barked at her.

"Who are *you*?" Fern barked back.

"This is our boat, you're the one who's trespassing!"

"This is a free sea!" said Fern. "Anyone can go for a swim."

"They can indeed." The boy turned to the others. "So let's throw her back, shall we?" The others closed in on Fern, who had nowhere to back away. One of the girls, an angelic little nine-year-old with brown ringlets grabbed Fern's backpack from her.

"Give that back," yelled Fern.

"Open it, Lulu," the leader said to the girl.

Lulu dumped the contents of the backpack out on the deck. She rifled through everything, announcing each object for the leader. "Maps, compass, atlas, botany book . . ."

"What's all that for?" the leader asked.

Fern was silent.

"Don't play games with me!" said the boy. "Answer my question."

"Why do you want to hurt me? I haven't done anything to you!"

"No . . . except you've seen us. You know where we are, and you're probably just some stupid little runaway whose mommy and daddy are going to be traipsing after you at any moment. You should go back where you came from . . . now!" Lulu and Kai and the others closed in on Fern. They grabbed her arms and legs and lifted her off the deck. Fern kicked and fought. They carried her to the side of the boat.

"Don't do this!" begged Fern, knowing she needed to stay on the *Porpoise* to discover who or what had cried out to her for help. "No one's coming after me . . . I won't tell anyone about you. I don't even know who you are!"

"Throw her back," said the leader.

The kids looked apprehensively at him. After all, she was just a kid, and it was a big, dark ocean.

They began to lower her toward the choppy water.

"Go on!" he ordered.

Fern was inches from the sea when a voice rang out from the deck of the boat.

"Anthony! Stop it!"

The golden-haired boy looked back over his shoulder toward the voice. He lowered the harpoon.

"Why?" he asked. Just then an orange-haired girl emerged into the moonlight; a fair-skinned orange-haired girl.

"Because that's Fern Verdant, the girl who helped me escape from NITPIC," she answered. Fern looked up, very surprised to recognize Francesca.

Francesca

Fern was hauled back onto the deck. Anthony trained his harpoon on the end of her nose.

"Anthony!" Francesca helped Fern to her feet.

Anthony reluctantly lowered his weapon. Fern was shaking so hard from the cold that she could barely speak. Her teeth chattered wildly.

"She's freezing!" Francesca wrapped a blanket around Fern.

"Th-th-thanks." Fern looked down. Bits of seaweed hung off her arms and legs. Strands of it were entwined in her hair.

"What are you doing here?" Anthony's eyes narrowed. Fern didn't know what to say. "Do you have parents?"

This was an upsetting question for Fern, for obvious reasons.

"I have a faraway father, and a missing mother."

"See! She's dangerous!"

"Please! Leave her alone, Anthony," said Francesca.

"Why? Even if she did help you, what is she doing here? Maybe she's a spy. Did you ever think of that? She obviously followed you to us!"

Fern thought about what she could say to defend herself. She didn't have to think long because a now-familiar sharp scissor-cry bit into her brain. Fern had only a moment to recognize it as the painful, disturbed plea that had led her to this boat. Weak, cold, and exhausted, Fern fell down unconscious.

The next morning Fern woke up below deck wearing dry, clean pajamas. The bits of seaweed had been picked from her hair. She felt drained, as would any person who'd lost their mom, run away, lived in a tree, hiked miles, swum out to sea, and been dangled in a net above the deck of a boat. Her head still hurt from the scream.

Francesca came below deck with some hot cocoa. "Are you feeling better?" She held out the steaming cup. "Drink this."

Fern was chilly, and gratefully sipped the cocoa. She admired the cabin, which was painted bright blue and green and pink. It smelled like fresh paint.

"I just painted it myself," said Francesca proudly.

"It's beautiful," said Fern.

"It's the first room I've ever had on my own."

From the way the boat was moving, Fern suspected they weren't just bobbing off shore anymore. She felt the warmth of the hot chocolate creeping through her whole body.

"Anthony is my brother," Francesca said. "I'm sorry if he

seemed mean yesterday, but he's very suspicious of everybody, especially non-orphans. All of us on board are orphans. He figures if a kid's not an orphan then there's going to be a parent snooping around and looking for it. Any grown-up who comes across a boatful of kids is going to report them, and then we'd get sent back to places like NITPIC or to orphanages."

"I don't want to turn anyone in anywhere." Fern sat up. "I just want to find my mother."

"Why did you swim out to *this* particular boat?" Francesca asked suspiciously.

This gift was forcing Fern to do something she had never done before; she was going to have to lie. Lily had always taught Fern to tell the truth as a child. This seemed odd now considering that Lily had hidden her own secret from the world. Was it a lie to simply not tell the truth, to withhold information? But this wasn't the time or place for philosophy.

"I ran away from NITPIC the same night you did. I saw you running across the fields. I didn't follow you, though . . . honestly I didn't. I had my own plan." Fern didn't bother filling Francesca in on the Eucalyptus. Instead, she said, "My mother is being held prisoner somewhere very far away. When I left NITPIC, I took a train to find her. I traveled until I ended up in Dollop, the tiny beach town you were anchored near. It's not easy being a thirteen-year-old traveling alone. There's a lot of discrimination. People want to know where your parents are, what you're doing, where you're going. There was a nosy, gross lifeguard after me in Dollop. I was afraid he'd turn me in as a runaway, so I stole his buoy and swam out to sea. I saw the beautiful fireworks above your boat. It seemed to me that anyone who set off such beautiful explosions might be friendly. So I swam here." Fern held her breath, wondering if Francesca would believe her.

"Those fireworks were definitely a bad idea." Anthony appeared in the doorway. "We were celebrating Francesca's return. What about that lifeguard? Did he see you swim out to this boat?"

"I don't know what he saw in the night from the shore."

Fern was quiet, waiting to see what Anthony was going to say or do next. It was obvious that he was the leader of this boat full of children, that they either respected him or feared him. Fern wasn't sure which. The *Porpoise* rose and fell on the swells of the sea. As it did, a cabin door swung open behind Anthony. Through the door Fern saw a glass box on a table. There was something shiny and silver in the box, something that practically blinded her. At first she couldn't make out what it was, then the longer she stared, the more she could see . . . it was a silver petal.

Fern gawked. She couldn't help it. The scratchy words itched into her head.

"Ferrrnnnn, iz it chew?" The Petal was speaking to her. Fern's mouth fell open. She knew from what Lily had said that there had only been one single Silver Rose in the whole world. This Petal had to be from that Rose. This Petal had been with her mother when she'd disappeared.

"It's me, Fern Verdant!" she blurted out aloud, forgetting

where she was. The Petal heard Fern, and Fern heard a sigh of relief.

"We already know who you are," responded Anthony.

"At lazt," the Petal sighed. "Thank goodnez." The voice no longer had a frantic, frightened tone. It was calmer, sounding more like a hiss or a whisper. Anthony followed Fern's gaze, to the glass box. The glint of silver flashed in his eyes. He slammed the door quickly, and exchanged a troubled look with his sister.

"That petal . . . it's from the Silver Rose, isn't it?"

They were all quiet.

"It can help me find my mother."

Anthony scowled. "You're very nosy for a person who snuck on board and shouldn't be here to begin with."

"Please, you have to listen to me." Fern told her story, at least as much of it as she could. "My mother is a botanist. She travels the world saving dying species. She disappeared when she went to help a Silver Rose developed by the horrible Hubrises. She was kidnapped. Your petal has to be from that same Silver Rose, since there was only one of them in the world."

"We're not stupid, you know!" Anthony barked back at her. "Where else would a Silver Petal come from, but a Silver Rose? We intend to find that Silver Rose. It would be very rare and very valuable. We'd sell it for a lot of money, then we could build a hideout, and no one will be able to separate us again." Anthony ducked back out of the cabin door. Then, as if having an afterthought, he stuck his head back in.

"Isn't it a remarkable 'coincidence' that you just happened

to swim to a boat that had a Silver Petal from your mother's last patient?" He squinted his eyes and scowled.

"Remarkable," said Fern.

"I don't know what you're up to, but as soon as you can stand up, we're putting you in a dinghy, and you can find your way home. We don't need a meddlesome spying non-orphan on this boat." Anthony slammed the cabin door as he left.

Francesca sat down with a sigh next to Fern's bed.

"It *is* a strange coincidence, but Anthony has a short fuse. He's been through some terrible times. I may have been at NIT-PIC, but Anthony"—Francesca shuddered—"has lived through horrors. I'm grateful that we're finally together." Francesca looked at Fern with meaning. "I won't do anything that would tear us apart again."

Fern got out of her bed, and started putting her clothes back on. She felt a little woozy, and had to sit down.

"There's no point in rushing, especially if you're just going to be put in a dinghy in the middle of the ocean," Francesca said. Fern could see the logic in that, and sat back down.

"Can I ask you a question?"

"It depends on the question," Francesca replied.

"Do you know where your brother found the Silver Petal?"

Francesca was quiet.

"Please," said Fern, "imagine if you knew your mother was alive and in danger. Wouldn't you do everything in your power to try and find her?"

Francesca seemed a little envious. Finally, she answered. "He found it when he ran away."

"Where did he run away from?" Fern pressed.

Fern could see Francesca was trying to figure out whether to trust her or not.

"When our parents died," started Francesca, "we were split up. Anthony was sent to live with a very distant relative, a cousin named Hamper Wesley. Hamper was a fisherman, up north. He only took Anthony in so he could have a slave. Hamper made Anthony sleep in a shed and do all of the homework for his three stupid sons. Anthony was forbidden to go to school himself. With my brother doing their work, the three sons started getting straight A's. They hated him for being smart, and so they beat him up all the time."

Francesca looked down at the floor. It was very difficult for her to have to repeat these stories out loud. "This went on for years. Anthony and I never knew where each other were."

"That's terrible!" said Fern.

"Anthony found out Hamper Wesley had a secret. He made bags of money by capturing rare Sapphire Dolphins and selling them illegally to aquariums in China. One night, Anthony released the dolphins back into the sea and took one of Hamper's boats, the very boat we're floating on now. He left behind a letter with duplicates of photographs of Hamper with the rare dolphins. He wrote that if anyone came after him, the authorities would be notified. Some homeless kids in town left with Anthony. They painted the boat orange to disguise it. Anthony found out I was at NITPIC and wrote to me, but Dr. Von Svenson took away the letters. She didn't know I'd already memorized the call number for the boat. The night I escaped,

Anthony was heading down the coast toward Nedlaw to break me out of NITPIC. Thank goodness you showed up and told me about the drugged milk. I might not have been able to escape otherwise."

"And the Silver Petal?" prodded Fern. "Where did he find the Silver Petal?" The door swung open, and Anthony stepped in.

"We have the dinghy ready. It's loaded with food, water, and your backpack. You should be fine."

"I really don't think she'll do us any harm," Francesca said.

"One parent on the lookout for a child, and we're sunk. It's too dangerous." Anthony disappeared up the stairs.

Fern got up. She hesitated by the open door to the galley, and caught a glimpse of the Silver Petal. Francesca hovered nearby.

"May I go in and look at the Petal?" Fern asked.

Francesca already felt pretty rotten about everything. "Just for a moment."

Fern stepped into the room. The delicate Silver Petal was battered, but beautiful. Fern whispered, "Do you know where my mother is?" She leaned in and listened closely. An answer grated into her head. Fern smiled.

Francesca stood waiting for Fern in the hall. "We'd better get going."

On deck Fern was met by gray sky and cool wind. The boat was headed out into the somber sea. Landfall lay behind them. Anthony had wasted no time in getting away from Dollop and the potentially hazardous lifeguard. The orphans stood around watching. Francesca sat unhappily. The dinghy slapped against the side of the boat.

"It's time," said Anthony.

"Please, let me join up with you. I'm sure I could be of some help." Fern's gaze was fixed on the endless horizon.

"You're not an orphan," Anthony said firmly. "You should go home."

This boy didn't understand Fern would never go home until she had found her mother.

"Now hurry up. You've got to get going," Anthony said.

Fern looked at him with a very determined expression.

"Don't dawdle!" he barked.

"I don't think you want to put me in that dinghy," Fern said.

"And why is that?" asked Anthony.

"Because." Fern paused here for dramatic effect. "I happen to know where the Silver Rose is, and you're going to need me to find it."

A Bargain

There's something called a Mexican standoff, presumably invented by some people in Mexico. It's when a lot of people are
all pointing guns at each other, and no one wants to shoot first
or everyone may get shot, and then no one will win. This was
kind of like that, a situation where no one knew what to believe
so everyone was stuck. It started with Francesca asking, "Do you
really know how to find the Silver Rose?"

"Yes. It's with my mother," answered Fern.

"She doesn't know where it is," said Anthony. "She's just
saying that so she can stay on this boat and take the Petal."

"I am not. I'm only trying to find my mother."

"How do we even know your mother is missing? It could all
be a big lie. You may just want the Silver Rose for yourself!"

"Fine. I'll prove it. Get my backpack!"

Anthony nodded to Lulu, who plucked the backpack out of the dinghy and handed it over. Fern pulled out the back issue of the *American Fern Journal* from where it was tucked into her mother's botany book. She flipped through it to the "Missing Botanists" section, and handed Anthony the article. "There . . . are you happy?"

Anthony looked at the picture of the missing Lily Verdant. There was no doubt this woman had to be Fern's mother. They looked like two peas in a pod. He read the article.

"Okay," said Anthony, "then where are they?"

Fern faltered for a minute. Truth be told, she had no idea where her mother was. The only thing she knew was what the Petal had said to her, and what the Petal had said to her was "We're heading in the right directzzzion, they're somewhere across the water."

When Fern found herself on deck heading toward open sea, she knew she needed to stay on that boat at any cost. She wouldn't get far out on the Pacific Ocean in a dinghy; besides, she wanted to have a real conversation with the Petal. That Petal was a floral witness to her mother's disappearance.

"I can't tell you—then you wouldn't need me. But I can lead you there. There is one important question I need to ask though. Can your boat cross an ocean?"

"Cross what?" Francesca said.

"My mother and the Rose are out there." Fern pointed across the prow of the boat, toward the horizon.

"You expect us to cross the ocean?" Anthony was intrigued. Imagine crossing a whole ocean. What an adventure!

"It's the safest place you could be. Hamper Wesley, the NIT-PIC security people, and Dr. Marita Von Svenson are never going to be searching out in the middle of the ocean!"

The safety of his crew and his sister were the most important things to Anthony, and Fern was right, the middle of the ocean was an excellent hiding place. If they found the Silver Rose, they'd be wealthy, and the lure of navigating the Pacific Ocean, the largest ocean in the world, was undeniable.

"Fine," said Anthony. "You'll lead us to the Silver Rose, but if you do anything suspicious, one little thing, it's into the dinghy with you. Only this time we'll be too far from shore for you to make it back alive."

"You'll be my roommate," Francesca said to Fern. "It'll be like having a sister. I never had a sister."

"Me neither," said Fern.

"Besides, then I can keep an eye on you." Francesca paused. "There's something you're not telling us, isn't there?" Fern hated fibbing so she said nothing at all.

That night Fern tried to stay awake until Francesca was asleep, but it was very difficult because Francesca was trying to stay awake until Fern fell asleep. They lay in their bunks with one eye open. Finally neither could stay awake any longer, and they both dozed off at the exact same moment.

Sleeping on a boat is an odd feeling if you've never done it before, and the rolling of the waves woke Fern up in the middle of the night. When she looked over, she saw that Francesca was fast asleep. Fern slid out of bed. Up on deck she could hear Anthony moving around. Francesca had told Fern that Anthony barely slept at all, that sometimes he just paced back and forth on the deck all night, keeping guard.

Fern pulled a sweater and jeans over her pajamas. She crept out of the dark cabin and into the galley where the Petal was kept. The rest of the crew was asleep. Fern closed the galley door behind her. In the middle of a long wooden table was the glass box that contained the Petal.

"Please," she whispered, "tell me what happened to my mother."

Fern knew the story of her mother's disappearance might be horrible, but she needed to know. The words came into Fern's head, with a gentle but sad hissing sound. The Silver Petal told the story of Lily's kindness to the Rose, of their escape, of the terrifying fall, and of the Petal's painful separation from the Rose.

"You sssszzzee," said the Silver Petal, "this Roszzze I'm part of is a freak, neither plant nor metal, but both. It's very lonely being a singular Silver Petal floating about in the world with no one to understand it."

Fern understood exactly how the Silver Petal felt. "Who passed the message from my mother to you?" she whispered.

"Seaweed," answered the Silver Petal. "I spent quite a bit of time being washed down the coastline. Several full moons shone on me. The message came one night clear as a bell. I passzt it on, and it found its way up the coast to you. I knew that wherever the message came from, that's where the Silver Rose was. There was no way for me to follow it. I was just a stupid, metal petal being pointlessly washed up on the beach and back

119

down to the shoreline with each and every tide. I had never been so bored in my life. Then the boy found me and brought me here. Now we can find my Roszzze and your mother. You can make them take us there!"

Fern and the Petal had arrived at the same conclusion. Fern knew she must next contact some seaweed and see about further information. She sat with the Petal for a while and whispered comforting thoughts. Then she went up on deck.

Anthony sat pensively in the moonlight, staring out to sea. He was startled when Fern emerged from the cabin below. He scowled in a way that asked, "What are you doing here?"

"I couldn't sleep."

Anthony turned his attention back to the ocean. He paced the length of the deck.

Fern whispered out over the waves, into the black night, down to the seaweed, "Please, can anyone down there tell me where Lily Verdant is?" Fern still felt a little weird talking to greenery.

"Did you say something?" Anthony turned to her.

Fern realized Anthony must think she was a little crazy for talking aloud to no one in particular, just like her father had thought she was unstable for chatting with a willow. She looked forward to the day when her telepathic abilities were realized and she wouldn't attract so much attention.

"No. It must have been the breeze." Fern listened hard for a response. The water was calm; the moonlight skipped over the surface in bright ripples. Fern saw pink and orange and green phosphorescent fish playing beneath the waves. Millions of stars speckled the night sky. She stared out at all the beauty. The world was becoming a magical place right in front of her eyes. The response came quickly. Only instead of from one single weed, it came from a whole bed, responding in languid voices.

"Your message traveled very far,
Across the waves
Beneath the stars
From flower and moss and trees and thus
Past coral reef, at last to us."

The voices seemed as though they were coming from very far away, and sounded lazy, as if the speakers could barely stay awake.

"Will you let me know when I'm near?" Fern whispered back.

"You'll know. You'll find us past the Doldrums," the voices drawled.

"Doldrums?"

Anthony turned around and looked at her suspiciously.

"What did you say?" Anthony was staring right at her. Fern was uncomfortable.

"Um . . . I said, 'the Doldrums' . . . I was just wondering about the Doldrums . . . out loud."

"We're nowhere near the Doldrums. We're too far north."

Any normal person would have explained more, but not Anthony. He had no clue about normal conversation.

"What are they?" asked Fern. Anthony ignored her. "You know, it's very rude to ignore someone asking you a question."

Anthony looked at her. Fern fidgeted. He made her feel like everything she said was silly and unimportant.

"Well, it's also very rude to climb on board someone's boat, uninvited, in the middle of the night." He had a point.

"Fine, I'll just go look up the Doldrums in one of your books."

"No need," said Anthony, who was fascinated by anything that had to do with the sea. Hamper Wesley had stacks of books about the ocean in his library, but he never opened any of them. At night, once everyone was asleep, Anthony would sneak into the library and read.

"The trade winds coming from the south and the north meet near the equator. The converging winds produce atmosphere that rises as it's heated, so there are no steady surface winds on the sea. That's the Doldrums. There's no wind. Boats don't sail. It's supposed to feel very, very creepy. Weirdly still. We don't have to worry, because we have an engine and plenty of gas."

Fern looked at Anthony, impressed.

"In the old days before engines, sailors died out there, starving to death because they couldn't get to land," Anthony added.

"Do you know practically everything about the ocean?"

Anthony made a noise, like a laugh. At least that's what Fern thought it was. His eyes sparkled slightly, the corners of his mouth turned up instead of down, and a little sound erupted from his throat.

"No."

"I bet you will someday," Fern said, turning back toward the stairs. Anthony watched as she went back down below deck.

"Hey!" he called out to her.

Fern stopped on the stairs. "Yes?"

"This isn't a cruise ship. You'll be helping with the chores while you're on board." Anthony regretted his momentary lapse into niceness, and had to make up for it somehow.

"No problem." And with that Fern disappeared below deck. Once she was back inside her bunk, she turned on the little overhead light and pulled her atlas out of her pack. Flipping through the pages, she stopped at the one that had the giant picture of the world spread out. On the North American side she figured out where Dollop was. Then she traced her finger down to the equator, across the huge Pacific Ocean, heading south, past the Doldrums to where the seaweed might be. Farther out there somewhere was the coral reef that the seaweed had mentioned. The coral reef must be far across the water in a sunny place like New Guinea or India or some other exotic location that Fern would never have imagined herself sailing to. She fell asleep thinking of palm trees, tropical breezes, and her mother.

The next morning Fern woke up feeling good. This was the first bed she'd slept in since she left Nedlaw, and that was five days ago, although it seemed like much more. In the galley everyone sat around eating breakfast, except for Anthony, who remained on deck.

"I think everyone should introduce themselves to Fern."

Francesca nodded to the other kids. None of them seemed too pleased to have Fern in their midst, even if she did know where the Silver Rose was. She wasn't an orphan, and they weren't sure they could trust her.

"I'm Lulu," said a slender girl with chestnut ringlets, who looked to be about nine. She wore overalls and was eating a banana.

A long-faced twelve-year-old boy looked up from a book he was studying. "Tim," he said, before returning his attention to a very complicated chart. "It's a map of ocean currents all around the world."

"Jane," piped up an eleven-year-old girl with blond hair, long legs, and a raspy voice.

The last one to speak was Kai. He was exotic-looking, and had beautiful almond-shaped green eyes. He was very slight, maybe seven or eight, with sun-bleached streaks in his soft brown hair and a long, thin scar on his cheek.

"Kai!" he blurted out. "And you better not bring any trouble to this boat, because it's the closest thing any of us have to a home."

"I don't want to bring trouble to anyone. In fact, I'd like to help. What chores can I do?" Fern asked the others.

They looked at one another. In unison, they cried, "Swab the deck!!!"

"Anthony is always yelling for someone to swab the deck . . . he's fanatical about it. He read about it in pirate books. Nobody wants to swab," Francesca said.

"Fine, I'd be happy to swab my way across the Pacific. It's

the least I can do to thank you all for helping me find my mother." Swabbing the deck would also provide a perfect opportunity for Fern to keep her eyes open for seaweed and to pick Anthony's brain about other useful seafaring tidbits. Fern smiled at them all. No one smiled back, except Francesca. Fern could see that this was not going to be a pleasant voyage.

Meanwhile

In the days following the big storm Olivier was beside himself. His conversation with Dr. Marita Von Svenson had left him feeling terrible. He missed his missing wife and he missed his sent-away daughter, and then to learn his daughter blamed him for Lily's disappearance! Feeling horrible one night, he picked up the phone and called Grandmamma Lisette.

It was very early in the morning when the phone rang in Paris, France, but Olivier knew Grandmamma would be up. Grandmamma always got up early to bake her exceptional chocolate croissants.

"*Bonjour,*" she chirped into the phone at five a.m. Paris time.

"I am not having a very 'bon jour.'" Olivier proceeded to

explain everything that had happened with Fern and how she was now a live-in patient at NITPIC.

"*Mon dieu!*" cried Grandmamma. "Talking to a tree?"

"*Oui,*" said Olivier.

"But Olivier, you talk to trees all the time."

"I know, but I don't expect them to answer. Now the psychiatrist says Fern blames me for Lily's disappearance."

Grandmamma was startled. This didn't sound right to her.

"But that is *très* odd. Fern told me that she blames herself for her missing mother."

Olivier was puzzled. Grandmamma told him she thought something was very fishy indeed. She urged Olivier to go to NITPIC and investigate. The next morning he got up and paced and worried. Dr. Von Svenson did seem intent on protecting Fern's welfare. He paced some more. It was a beautiful day, but he didn't really notice as he paced right out the front door, mumbling aloud to himself.

"Should I disobey the doctor's orders? Should I go to Fern? Will I be helping? Will I be hurting?" Olivier paced the length of the lawn, talking to himself. When he looked up, he found he was standing in front of the very tree that Fern had been talking to. In the driveway, Mr. Pertin, the postman, had stopped in his tracks on his way to the mailbox. He stared curiously at Olivier Verdant, who appeared to be talking to a tree.

"Good morning," said Olivier. Mr. Pertin tipped his hat cautiously, hurriedly dropped a bundle of mail in the mailbox, and then practically ran down the path to his mail truck.

"What on earth is wrong with our postman?" Olivier said to himself. He looked at the base of the scarred tree in front of him; the same tree Fern had talked to. It suddenly dawned on him that Mr. Pertin had been afraid of him because Olivier appeared to be talking to a tree! What if Fern had really just been talking to herself? Olivier was horrified.

The Verdant Volvo screeched into the NITPIC driveway. The place was in rough shape after the big storm. The Douglas firs that used to be tall and regal were now bent and depressed-looking. Inside, Olivier raced down the hall to Dr. Marita Von Svenson's office . . . except Dr. Marita Von Svenson's name was no longer on the door to her office. Instead, there was a sign that announced Dr. Vladislaw Linsky. Olivier searched up and down the hall, but Von Svenson's name was nowhere to be found. He knocked on the door to Dr. Vladislaw Linsky's office, which he could have sworn used to be Dr. Marita Von Svenson's office. A thickset, kindly man with a gray-flecked beard opened the door.

"Can I help you?" he asked.

"I'm looking for Dr. Marita Von Svenson," Olivier replied.

"No longer here, I'm afraid," Dr. Linsky replied in a slight Polish accent. "Left rather abruptly two days ago. I'm the emergency replacement. Dr. Vladislaw Linsky, psychiatrist." Dr. Linsky stuck out his hand to shake Olivier's. Olivier shook Dr. Linsky's hand.

"Olivier Verdant, botanist and bad parent. I'm here to rectify that. I don't suppose it will matter now if I take my daughter, Fern Verdant, home against Dr. Marita Von Svenson's wishes."

"I'm sorry." Dr. Linsky scratched his head. "But I don't believe there's anyone named Fern Verdant at this institute.".

Olivier had never heard anything so ridiculous in his life. This Dr. Linsky didn't even know who his patients were.

"I checked her in here myself five days ago."

"Let me look into this." The doctor did not want to upset Olivier any further. "After all, I only just arrived yesterday. I've been memorizing the patient list, but could have easily overlooked one name." Dr. Linsky went to the computer and typed in Fern's name. Nothing. He rifled through the patient files. No Verdant. He turned to Olivier, rather concerned. Either Olivier Verdant was not very well, and perhaps in need of a stay at NITPIC's nearby adult facility, NITPIG (the Nedlaw Institute for the Treatment and Prevention of Insanity in Grown-Ups), or something was terribly, terribly wrong.

Down the hall Olivier noticed Mr. Carruthers.

"Where's my daughter?" Olivier grabbed Mr. Carruthers' arm.

"Who?"

"Fern Verdant! You checked her in here five days ago."

"Fern Verdant?" Carruthers stared blankly. "Who's Fern Verdant?"

Olivier was beside himself. Dr. Linsky was worried, very worried indeed. Linsky looked closely into Carruthers' eyes. He looked around at the children and the staff milling about the NITPIC halls. A grim realization dawned upon him. He turned to Olivier Verdant.

"I don't want to frighten you, but in my professional opinion, every person in the NITPIC facility has been hypnotized."

The Nedlaw police arrived within half an hour. Everyone was questioned, but no one had ever heard of, or seen, Fern Verdant. Dr. Linsky tried hard to un-hypnotize everyone, but he wasn't familiar with Dr. Marita Von Svenson's powerful techniques. Even Beatrice Minx, the assistant Linsky had inherited, was hypnotized. At first the police were a little suspicious of Olivier. After all, he'd had a missing wife, and now a missing daughter. They thought it odd that he kept losing his family. However, as soon as they saw how frantic he was, they eliminated him as a suspect in the disappearance of Fern Verdant.

The police put out an alert. Fern's picture was sent up and down the coast and all over the countryside. Scrawled under her name were the words *Have you seen this girl?*

Olivier spent the day answering questions at the police station. Late that night he drove up to the Verdant home. On the way in, Olivier picked up the mail that Mr. Pertin had dropped off that morning. Among the bills and junk mail was a letter addressed to him in Fern's writing. Olivier tore open the envelope that Beatrice Minx had accidentally held hostage in her satchel.

Dear Dad,

    I have run away from NITPIC because I have something very, very important to do. I am going to find Mom. I know she's alive. Please don't worry about me. I want you to trust me, and don't try to follow me, or bad

things will happen. I love you more than
anything. I will call you.

xoxoxoxox, Fern

P.S. Dr. Marita Von Svenson is evil. The kids
at NITPIC are all drugged, and they walk
around like they're half-dead. Please contact
the authorities, and have them look into it.

Olivier called Grandmamma Lisette immediately and read her the letter.

"*Mon Dieu!*" Grandmamma couldn't believe her ears. "Are you going to give the letter to the police?" she asked.

Many thoughts were crossing Olivier's mind.

"I don't think so," he finally answered. "If the police think she's been abducted, they'll look harder for her than if they think she's just a crazy runaway." Olivier slumped down into a chair. "I'll tell you one thing, I'm not going to just sit around and wait. I'm going to find Fern myself. I can't go on losing my family like this."

There was silence on the other end of the telephone as Grandmamma considered her next words very carefully. "You don't think it's possible . . . that maybe . . . Lily is alive?" The question snapped Olivier to attention.

"Of course not. If she were, she'd never stay away from us for this long."

"I'm catching the next flight over there," Grandmamma

said. Olivier agreed, wanting what was left of his family to be in one place.

The next morning the police came by the Verdant home to say that a fat, tattooed lifeguard named Big Dog, who should not be allowed to wear a Speedo swimsuit, had reported seeing Fern in the tiny beach town of Dollop. Big Dog hadn't told them about seeing Fern swim out to sea; after all, they would have wondered why he had not rescued her. He said he'd seen her briefly on the beach, then she'd disappeared. He was annoyed to learn there was no reward. The police reassured Olivier that they'd call if something else popped up.

Grandmamma arrived the next day.

"I'm going to find Dr. Marita Von Svenson," Olivier told Grandmamma. "She's involved in this. Why else would she hypnotize the memory of Fern out of everyone's heads, and then disappear?" Grandmamma agreed. She was quite tired after her long flight, and went to bed early.

Olivier sat up alone, trying hard not to think about the possibility that his wife was still alive. It would be too painful to believe it, and then find out it wasn't true. But Fern's note nagged at him. He called the home of Claude and Luella Hubris. The phone rang endlessly. Then a recorded voice announced that that number was out of service. He called the local sheriff, whom he'd become acquainted with when Lily first went missing. He learned the Hubrises had simply disappeared from their rented house months ago. For the first time in ages Olivier let himself entertain the thought that his wife might still be alive.

Trouble

The *Porpoise* was a fishing boat, not a speedboat. It didn't move very fast, and it was powered by an engine, so there were no sails to hoist and nothing you could do to speed up its putt-putt-putting across the water. All you could do was point it in the right direction and then find ways to spend your time.

Anthony had stocked the *Porpoise* with food and water, gasoline, and other essentials for life at sea. He had also stocked it with books taken from Hamper's library. Each day he made sure that the *Porpoise*'s crew had a lesson. Francesca was their teacher. Everybody's favorite subject was geography. Since they were traveling around the world themselves, they felt like they were living their lesson. Lessons were only a part of their day, though. Chores made up the rest.

Tim was in charge of navigation. He pored over books,

maps, and charts, analyzing exactly where they were and where they were going. Lulu was the cook. Among the books on board the boat was *The Joy of Maritime Cooking, or 1,001 Ways to Prepare a Flounder*. Lulu hated cooking fish and couldn't find one ounce of joy in it. She invented forty ways to serve oatmeal, including an oatmeal souffle that everyone agreed was delicious. Kai fished, so sometimes Lulu had to prepare his catch. She wore a nose plug on those occasions. Jane entertained everyone with wonderful stories. She loved to read, and made up tales that featured the orphans as the protagonists.

Fern kept a very low profile on board the boat. Swabbing the decks took up a lot of her time. The others didn't trust her or speak to her. Her only ally was Francesca, and Francesca had been warned by Anthony to be careful and not get too chummy with their passenger. In the evening, when the others were doing their schoolwork, Fern would retire to her cabin and read her mother's botany book. She figured if she was going to be talking to plants, she'd better know something about them.

By her second day at sea, Fern's routine was established. From dawn to dusk she swabbed. After dinner, when Francesca thought everyone else was asleep, she asked Fern questions about her parents, as if she was inquiring about some exotic species. Fern felt bad when she spoke to Francesca about Olivier and Lily, because she thought it made Francesca feel sad that she didn't have parents of her own.

During the day, as Fern swabbed, she asked Anthony about sailing and the sea. He answered in gruff one-word replies. He was determined to set an example of unfriendliness. The other shipmates did as he did. It made for a lonely time for Fern, and she had to remind herself that she was not here to make friends, but to save her mother. She did chat with the Petal, but it had only one story to tell. You can only listen to the same story so many times, even if your mother is the main character.

Each day as she swabbed the deck, Fern looked overboard and whispered to the seaweed, asking if the *Porpoise* was heading in the right direction. The seaweed formed itself into the shape of an arrow, and pointed out the direction that the *Porpoise* should steer in. Any adjustment in course was passed along to Anthony. One day Anthony hid and watched Fern talking to the ripples on the surface of the sea. Unbeknownst to him, on this particular day, the *Porpoise* was above a patch of especially well-informed seaweed; the same seaweed that the Hubrises had sailed over months before. The arrow indicated that a sharp turn to the south was required. Fern whispered "thanks" and went to find Anthony.

Anthony stepped out from his hiding place and peered over the side of the boat. There he saw a patch of seaweed in the shape of an arrow. When Anthony's shadow loomed over the water, the arrow immediately disassembled, and the seaweed tried to look as nonchalant as possible. Fern found Anthony leaning over the side of the boat. He looked up suspiciously. She looked at him suspiciously.

"We need to steer the *Porpoise* that way," she said, pointing.

"Exactly how are you getting this information?" he asked.

"I can't tell you . . . but please, just trust me." There was dead silence as they stared at each other. Anthony didn't trust her.

Every time she looked overboard seeking direction from the seaweed, Fern noticed something. In the wake of the fishing boat she saw oily streaks seeping into the ocean from the engine of the *Porpoise*. The phosphorescent spillage clung to the seaweed. They coughed and sputtered as they formed their arrows. It was very disturbing, but Fern didn't know what to do about it.

As the boat sailed farther out to sea, Fern became interested in Tim's work. She watched over his shoulder as he charted their progress on a big map of the Pacific Ocean. She could see the *Porpoise* inching its way across the vast blueness.

"If we keep going in this direction, where will we end up?"

"There are hundreds of places out there," he said, pointing at the map. "Anywhere in the southeast Pacific and beyond. It depends on how far we go." Fern still had no idea how far they would be going.

Whenever Fern chatted with Tim, Anthony wanted to know all the details. Each member of the crew had to report any conversation they had with Fern, even if it was about something silly, like their favorite flavor of ice cream. Francesca was devoted to her brother, but she couldn't help feeling Fern meant them no harm.

One day, Anthony came to Fern while she was busy swabbing. He was very friendly—too friendly. Fern was wary, since Anthony had never disguised his dislike for her.

"I have a favor to ask you. We're having an 'all hands'

meeting. I need you to stay up there and be our lookout since you're not really part of the permanent crew. Can you keep your eyes peeled and let us know if anything unusual happens?"

Fern didn't trust this one bit, but what could she say except, "Of course I'll be lookout. I said I'd help any way I could." Fern climbed up into the bridge, which held the controls for the fishing boat. It was elevated above the deck, and from it you could see the great expanse of ocean. The sun shone, and the water rose and fell in gentle swells.

"It's beautiful up here." Fern tried to keep the hint of suspicion out of her voice.

"I'll come back up when we're done. It should only be half an hour or so. It'll probably be quiet, but this is the ocean. Things come out of nowhere. Never take your eyes off the horizon. Got it?"

"Got it," answered Fern. Anthony disappeared with all the others. Fern suspected their meeting was probably about her. She was right.

Anthony ordered the others below deck to Francesca's room. He was determined to find out more about Fern Verdant.

"Don't leave any stone unturned," he ordered. Anthony dumped everything out of Fern's backpack. He, Jane, Lulu, Tim, and Kai started tearing through her belongings. Francesca just watched, uneasy about this search. They thumbed through every single page of Lily's botany book. They tore open the remaining energy bars. Anthony reread the article in the *American Fern Journal* about Fern's missing mother.

"There's got to be a clue here somewhere! Something that

will tell us about this girl and her bizarre behavior." But search as they might . . . they found nothing. Anthony sighed. Francesca gave him a look that said, "I told you so." Kai took a bite of an energy bar.

"Nasty," he announced, spitting it across the room.

Tim studied Fern's atlas. Lulu asked if she could return to the business of preparing lunch. Jane had been helping her make oatmeal cakes. Anthony was frustrated. He was sure there was something fishy going on here. He picked up the backpack again, and shook it angrily. Nothing. He jammed his hand deep into it, and felt in all the corners. Nothing. Nothing . . . then . . . something! It was attached to one of the corners of one of the pockets.

"What's this?" Anthony turned the backpack inside out to get a better look at whatever it was. Whatever it was, it was held secure by a little metal wire. "Tim, get me some wire cutters and a magnifying glass."

It was a tiny piece of plastic-encased electronic equipment. A red light flashed sporadically. Tim returned with the wire cutters and the magnifying glass. Anthony freed the little plastic widget. It was in the shape of an eyeball. He could see teeny words printed on the side, but they were too small to read. He took the magnifying glass. Through it the words grew larger.

" 'Unbelievably Strong Electronic Tracking Device. Property of NITPIC. Do not remove or we will be very angry,' " he read aloud.

Anthony lowered the magnifying glass and looked at his crew, who had lost any hint of color from their faces.

"I knew it!" He stormed out of the cabin and headed up the stairs toward the bridge. The entire crew trailed after Anthony. Francesca lagged behind, horribly disappointed. She couldn't believe Fern would do this to them. Anthony burst into the bridge.

"How dare you spy on us for NITPIC!" Anthony was furious.

Fern didn't hear him. Her attention was focused out to sea, and she was completely mesmerized. Anthony followed her gaze. His mouth fell open in shock. The rest of the orphans tumbled up after him. A couple of hundred feet ahead of them was the strangest sight that any of the crew had ever seen. It looked like a green wall. It was about thirty feet high and twenty feet long. It undulated with the rhythm of the waves, like a mossy blanket someone was gently shaking. It appeared to be . . . a wall of algae. The *Porpoise*, still on automatic pilot, was chugging right toward it. Anthony pushed Fern out of the way. He turned the wheel of the boat to avoid the giant green wall. It was impossible to tell if it was hard or soft, if the boat would bounce off of it or go right through it and be slimed in the green goop. When Anthony steered the boat away, the green wall moved, blocking the *Porpoise*'s progress. It was engaged in a creepy dance, with the *Porpoise* leading, and the slime following.

"Why didn't you call me?" Anthony yelled.

"Because it appeared just before you did!" Fern cried. Fern hadn't even had a moment to talk with the algae.

"What's this?" Anthony demanded, holding out the device. Fern reached for the blinking device, but Anthony held on to it.

"I don't know. What is it?"

"It's a tracking device." Fern was in shock. "It's from NIT-PIC," he added, cutting the engines of the *Porpoise*, "and it was in your backpack." The *Porpoise* bobbed on the ocean, not going anywhere.

"That's not possible!" Fern cried out, wondering how on earth it could have ended up there. Had she unwittingly led Dr. Marita Von Svenson out here in the middle of nowhere to the orphans' doorstep?

"I didn't know it was there!" cried Fern.

"Even if I believed that, which I don't, you've still placed us all in danger," shouted Anthony. The crew was furious. Anthony pointed toward the green wall facing them.

"And I'm sure that has something to do with you," he added.

Just then Francesca raced up from below deck. "Wait, Anthony! What if Fern didn't know the device was in there? What if . . ." Francesca's voice trailed off as she noticed something glinting out of the corner of her eye. It was the sun reflecting off the metal hull of a boat in the distance . . . a boat moving super-fast toward the stern of the *Porpoise*. Its hull looked like a fishy snout. Francesca picked up a pair of binoculars and focused them on the vessel. *The Barracuda* was written on its side. Then she tilted the binoculars upward. Francesca was shocked when she recognized the black leather–clad figure of Dr. Marita Von Svenson standing on the deck of the swiftly approaching boat.

Meanwhile #2

What on earth could Olivier Verdant, a botanist specializing in ferns, do in the face of all this adversity? He tried to hide his emotions, but truth be told, he was heartbroken when Fern began to fall apart. He had felt useless and spent a great deal of time, like many other Frenchmen, staring mysteriously into space. But as soon as Olivier discovered that everyone at NIT-PIC had been hypnotized by Dr. Marita Von Svenson, that the horrible Hubrises had disappeared, and that Fern had run away because she believed her mother was still alive, Olivier became a man of action.

He pieced together the clues surrounding his family's disappearance. After the sighting by the overweight lifeguard from Dollop, Fern had evaporated.

"How coincidental," said Olivier to Grandmamma, "that

both my wife and daughter disappeared at the ocean's edge." He admitted to her that he believed there was a possibility Lily could be alive.

"Why would someone want to kidnap Lily?" Grandmamma mused. "She's a wonderful botanist, but kidnapping seems extreme!"

"There's no note. No ransom. Very peculiar!" Olivier said. "I'm going to search the world until I find them."

Grandmamma felt the pain and suffering of her son. She fell into deep and silent thought for a few minutes.

"Sit down, Olivier. There are some things I must tell you." She looked very serious. "Things I had never planned to tell you, about your father and me. I think it might be important to do so now."

Olivier sat down, unprepared for what was about to come next. Grandmamma took a big breath.

"Many years ago," she began, "I was part of a very secret society called the 'Resistance.' We resisted anything that was bad or evil. We skulked around in trench coats, having secret meetings, using strange passwords, trying to eliminate evil in the world. We tried our best to get rid of the bad and protect the good. It was very dangerous." Olivier's mouth fell open.

"You were . . . a spy . . . ?"

"Actually, more like a secret agent. I learned how to fly a plane and pilot a submarine. And once, undercover"—Grandmamma allowed herself a giggle—"I posed as an ostrich-back-riding polo player in Argentina. I was very good at bareback ostrich riding, and even took it up as a hobby for a while." Olivier's mouth had practically come unhinged.

"I was young, and it was a very adventurous way to live. All of this was great fun until I fell in love with, and married, a dashing and handsome fellow agent—your father, Luc Verdant."

"My mother *and* my father were secret agents!" Olivier was incredulous.

"*Oui*, your father was as famous as he could be without blowing his cover. He was nicknamed *L'Homme Invisible*. The Invisible Man. Luc trained as a botanist, just like you, and he used that cover to protect his secret-agenting life. I opened a bakery. We botanied and baked and agented together quite happily. After your birth I refused to agent anymore. It was too dangerous. Luc loved it and couldn't give it up. It was in his blood. One day, when you were four years old, your father was sent to South America to stop an evil dictator. He was killed." Grandmamma had to pull herself together. The thought of her husband's death still upset her to this day. Olivier was stunned. He'd always been told that his father had died in a freak bicycling accident on the Rue du Football.

"It was the saddest funeral, because although he was loved and respected by all the agents of the world, none could come pay their respects for fear of blowing their cover. You and I were the only visible people at the gravesite. A few other friends came, but they had to hide in the trees. From that day forth I swore I would never have anything to do with the world of the Resistance, and I didn't."

Olivier listened intently. He was shocked.

"I'm telling you this for a reason. One of my old co-agents, Serge Cransac, is now the head of the Resistance. Perhaps he can help you in your search."

Olivier stared off into space. It was as though he had just learned his mother was from the moon.

"So," continued Grandmamma, "if you want them to help us, just say the word."

"Us?" Olivier snapped to. "Mama, you are not going anywhere!"

"B-b-but . . . ," stammered Grandmamma.

"No buts. I will accept any help Serge Cransac can give, but I am not placing another member of my family in jeopardy. Besides, what if Fern or Lily sent a message or even came home? Someone must be here to meet them." Olivier hugged his mother. While she was not particularly thrilled at the prospect of her son going off alone, Grandmamma understood.

"Then you must promise me that you won't do anything without the help of Serge Cransac."

Olivier nodded. It was the least he could do.

Prisoner #2

Francesca screamed as the *Barracuda* bore down on the *Porpoise*. Anthony followed her gaze and saw the boat. Before the startled orphans could blink, the *Barracuda* was upon them. A stern-looking blonde stood on the deck of the quickly approaching boat. On either side of her were two huge muscle-bound men.

"It's Dr. Marita Von Svenson," whispered Francesca. Anthony was half expecting this. In front of the *Porpoise*, the green wall of algae blocked their passage into the Pacific. Behind them, the crazy psychiatrist was closing in. The *Porpoise* bobbed in the waves, helpless.

"Algae! Algae! Get out of the way! Let us get by! Please!" Fern whispered urgently.

"Not on your life, sister!" the Algae answered telepathically. They snickered en masse. "We don't need you saving plants. We need all the room on this planet we can get. The more plants that croak, the better for us. Now, get lost!!" Anthony watched Fern talking to the green wall. Maybe she really had belonged in NITPIC? He barely had time to consider the thought before Dr. Marita Von Svenson and the *Barracuda* were upon them. Anthony pushed Fern away from the *Porpoise*'s bridge.

"I hope you're happy!" He jammed the boat's throttle down as far as it would go. The *Porpoise* started moving away from the *Barracuda*, chugging south, parallel to the algae wall. There was no competition between the two boats. A big lump of a man on board the *Barracuda* shot a metal hook attached to a rope at the *Porpoise*. The device clamped onto its side, securing it to the *Barracuda*. The man reeled in the *Porpoise* like a cumbersome fish. The two boats were now locked together. Fern felt terrible; she had unwittingly delivered a boat full of orphans to the mad psychiatrist. Marita, flanked by two bulky flunkies, was now boarding.

"Get off this boat!" Fern yelled as Marita stepped toward her. The psychiatrist noticed Fern's backpack on the deck.

"Where's my homing device?" she asked, rummaging around the knapsack. Anthony pulled it out of his pocket and held it up.

"You mean this?" he asked. Marita put out her hand. Anthony leaned toward her, as though he was going to hand it to her, and then tossed it overboard.

"Big deal," said Marita. "There's more where that came from. Technology is a wonderful thing, don't you think so, children?"

"You have no right to be here," Fern shouted. "Leave these kids alone!"

"You think you can just kidnap a boatload of orphans and no one's going to do a thing about it?" Anthony growled. "*You* are crazy!"

"What would I want with a stinking boatload of orphans?" Dr. Von Svenson laughed at the half-dozen puzzled faces staring at her.

"I don't want you . . . nobody wants you. I bet no one's ever even tried to adopt any of you. Do you think that's just a coincidence?" She smirked at the crew. "No, it's because you're rotten." Lulu looked like she was going to cry. Kai looked defiant. Tim and Jane had developed a thick skin—nothing got through to them, or at least they never showed it—but even they were visibly shocked by this cruelty.

"How boring do you think it is to hear the same complaints all the time? 'Oh, my mommy and daddy are dead . . . boo hoo hoo. Nobody loves me!' You're spineless, whiny little brats."

Anthony had heard just about enough. He marched up to her.

"Fine. Get off our boat, you evil witch."

Marita squinted in his direction. "I will, when I get what I came for." With that she nodded toward her crew of hulking henchthugs. One thick-necked brute lifted Anthony and hurled him across the deck.

Two others leapt forward and seized Fern. They swept her off her feet, her legs dangling in the air. She kicked one of the henchthugs in his shins, but he was a big lummox and barely felt it.

"Don't you hurt her!" Francesca warned. Anthony scrambled to his feet and put his arm around his sister, pulling her away from Marita. The minions charged forward into the bridge, wielding hammers. They destroyed it in moments. Bits of dials, controls, and gauges covered the floor. The throttle was ripped out of its base and hurled overboard. Fern watched, dangling, helpless and angry.

"Check the rest of this wreck, and see if there's anything else worth taking. Don't forget little Fern's belongings. There may be something interesting among them." Fern had a horrible suspicion that she knew why Marita Von Svenson was after her. There was a lot of crashing and banging below deck. One of the henchthugs lumbered back up carrying Fern's books and personal effects. Another henchthug followed, very proudly holding out the Silver Rose Petal. Marita smirked. She was obviously having an exceptionally good day.

"My goodness." Marita grabbed the Silver Petal, admiring it. "An embarrassment of riches."

Anthony lunged for the Petal. "You can't .take that. It's ours."

"It belongs to them," Fern cried. "Take me, but leave the Petal."

"Ohhh, must be an important little Petal if you're all so concerned about it!" Marita ordered her henchthugs, "Load it all onto the *Barracuda*, and let's get going." She turned to leave, and then, as if having a second thought, she squinted toward the algae wall and nodded in Fern's direction. "I hear you're supposed to have a special talent of some kind, can't you get rid of that thing?"

Fern felt sick. How on earth did Dr. Marita Von Svenson know she had a gift? The orphans watched, confused. Anthony was particularly curious.

Fern looked blankly at Marita. "I don't know what you're talking about. I think you might consider getting some professional help yourself."

"Stubbornness is such an ugly trait in a child. Put her on the *Barracuda*." The orphans watched as Marita's slimy sidekicks tossed Fern onto the sleek gray boat. Fern fell hard and hit her head. She felt woozy.

"Now," said Marita, "be careful. We want her alive and not too badly bruised. We have a long trip ahead of us."

The minions retreated onto the *Barracuda*. Von Svenson lingered, turning back to face the green wall. She pulled a peculiar-looking weapon out of her pocket. It was shaped like a gun. She raised it and pointed it. A silvery, frosty vapor flew from the "barrel" of the curious weapon and shot across the heads of the orphans, who all dropped to the floor of the *Porpoise*. It continued right over them, disinterested, and headed toward the algae wall. The vapor embraced every square inch of the wall. The algae turned hazy, as if it were coated in fog. It became denser and denser until, *snap!* It was now a wall of green ice, separating the *Porpoise* and the *Barracuda* from the rest of the ocean. Dr. Marita Von Svenson raised her weapon again. This time she fired from a second barrel, and a rubber bullet sped through the air. It shattered the algae ice into a million pieces that collapsed, tinkling, back into the sea. The western Pacific was revealed once more, like a blue welcome mat to a far-off land.

"Well then. Enough dawdling, let's get going." Then Marita had another thought. "Ooops! Forgot something. And I'm usually so good at multitasking." With that one of the henchthugs tossed her a lighter and some lighter fluid. She picked up a nearby rag and sprayed it with the fluid, setting it ablaze. Marita dropped the ball of fire onto the *Porpoise*'s deck. The deck burst into flames. Anthony made a move to extinguish them, but when he looked up Marita was pointing the Vapor-icer at him.

"Which do you think is worse," she asked, "being orphan toast or an orphan-sicle?" Anthony backed off. "Loose ends always unravel perfectly good evil plots."

The minions unhooked the line connecting the two boats. The engines of the *Barracuda* revved into action, and the boat pulled away. Fern watched, horrified, as the orphans grabbed anything at hand, scooping water out of the sea in an effort to douse the blaze on the *Porpoise*'s deck.

"You will not get away with this!" Anthony shouted at the *Barracuda* as it cut through the shards of rapidly melting algae. The immobilized *Porpoise* bobbed in the vast blue ocean. Fern slid one foot over the side of the *Barracuda*. Her toe had just grazed the water when she was yanked back by the scruff of her neck. A henchthug dragged Fern below deck and tossed her onto a bunk in a cabin. The Silver Petal was placed on a table beside her, and then the door was slammed shut and locked.

"What do you want with me? Where are you taking me?" Fern shouted. There was silence from the other side of the door. Fern heard the boots of the henchthugs clomping up the stairs, thumping above her on the deck. She felt the *Barracuda* accelerate to full throttle, and the boat bounced over the waves, heading to who-knew-where.

Fern was furious. She was also terrified for the *Porpoise* and its crew. A single small porthole afforded Fern her only glimpse outside. Through it she saw that the *Barracuda* was moving quickly away from the *Porpoise*, out into the Pacific Ocean. The flames on the *Porpoise* were rising higher and higher. The orphans were tossing the sealed gas cans overboard to prevent an explosion. Fern had to do something quickly. She flung open the small round window. Spray from the waves spritzed her face. Leaning out, she looked down at the sea.

"Seaweed!" she screamed out, her voice competing with the *Barracuda*'s engine. "Quick! It's an emergency! Save the *Porpoise*! Put out the fire!"

The seaweed shuddered and shook, and then disappeared below the waves. Behind Fern, the door to her cabin opened, and one of the henchthugs entered.

"Get away from that window," said a tall, square, and swarthy henchthug with a nametag that read *Oren*. Oren picked Fern up by the back of her shirt and dragged her out of the room. Fern kicked, and this time she aimed a little higher. He let out a howl and started shaking her wildly.

"Remember, I'm supposed to be kept alive!" Fern's voice sounded wobbly because Oren was shaking her so hard.

"Oren!" Marita's voice sliced through the sea air. His face scrunched in pain like an old potato, Oren dropped his prisoner on the deck. Fern snuck a quick look back to the *Porpoise*. A ripple was moving along the surface of the water toward the vessel. A waterspout rose from the ocean. The Seaweed whipped the water into a frenzied spray that soaked the boat and extinguished the flames. The orphans watched, incredulous and grateful. Puffs of smoke spiraled off the deck as the flames ebbed. The sopping crew collapsed with relief.

"There will be no more sticking your head out of portholes, Miss Verdant! While you are in my care you will do exactly as I say. Think of us as a floating NITPIC."

"Where are you taking me?" asked Fern.

"None of your business. Lock her away!"

The henchthugs dragged Fern below deck and put her and the Silver Petal in a small, dark cabin. She heard a series of locks slam shut behind her. Fern looked around. She was in a box of a room. There were no windows. It was just like a prison.

The Littlest Chapter

Olivier Verdant e-mailed every botanist he knew, sharing his suspicions that his wife might be alive. Lily Verdant was very well loved, and the idea that she might not be dead filled everyone with joy. All the botanists promised they would keep their eyes and ears open for any unusual botanical activity that might hint at Lily's whereabouts.

Grandmamma Lisette telephoned the International Headquarters of the Resistance. Serge Cransac answered. When he recognized the voice of Lisette Verdant on the other end of the phone, his face lit up like the sky on Bastille Day. Many years ago Serge had worked very closely with Luc and Lisette. He was heartbroken when Luc died and devastated when Lisette shut herself away from her undercover friends to ensure the safety of her son. But he respected her decision. After a few initial pleas-antries, Lisette got to the point.

"I need your help, Serge. I need information and equip-ment." Olivier was surprised by the tone in his mother's voice. This was not the mother he knew! It was as though Lisette had never left spying. Serge said that of course he would help Lisette find her granddaughter and daughter-in-law, and that all of the resources of the Resistance would be utilized to help his dear old friend. He would put himself personally at her disposal. Lisette put Olivier on the telephone with Serge.

"*Mon Dieu!*" exclaimed Serge. "I have not seen you since you were the tiniest little boy."

"*Bonjour,*" said Olivier. "It is so kind of you to help us."

"Anything for Lisette," answered Serge. "She was quite an agent in her day."

"There is one thing I am certain I must do in order to find my family. I need to locate Dr. Marita Von Svenson, Swedish doctor of psychiatry and tormentor of children. If I can find her, the truth about my wife and daughter will not be far behind."

"Anything I can do to help the Verdants, I will," answered Serge. "I will be in touch very soon." With that, he rang off the line. Olivier and Grandmamma Lisette exchanged a look that hinted of hope.

Mr. Saagwalla's Dream Come True

The walls were damp in the cave in Sri Lanka where Henry Saagwalla kept Lily Verdant. Since his arrival, Saagwalla had been performing experiments on Lily, looking for clues that would tell him more about her gift. Some days he would stick needles in her head, or in her feet, or any other place that amused him. Lily felt the needles, but couldn't even utter a cry. The Silver Rose was horrified.

There was no sunlight in the dark cave, so there was no plant life. The only plant in the cave was the Silver Rose, which didn't exactly qualify as a real plant anymore. It was mostly metal and shiny and brittle. A grow light kept the planty part of it planty. Lichen and moss were kept at bay by the encroaching darkness. This was a blessing for Lily, since most lichen and moss were the kind of plants that hoped her health might take a turn for the worse. They certainly didn't need any help surviving, and they thought that any plant that did was weak and pathetic: "survival of the fittest," they'd say in conversation.

Lily could not move, but she could think, and she had a very active mind. She worried about her daughter, she missed her husband, and she worried about all the endangered plants she was unable to help. The Silver Rose talked with Lily about the horrible Hubrises and Henry Saagwalla. Lily knew Saagwalla suspected her gift. He had to. Everything he did destroyed nature. Everything Lily did preserved it. It was obvious to Lily that Saagwalla had captured her in order to use her extraordinary and beautiful gift to further his own nature-destroying plans.

Lily and the Rose also discussed the Chia Man, who acted as a messenger between Saagwalla's house and the Hubrises. The Hubrises had opted to stay in the cave after Saagwalla's arrival because Luella wanted to be as far away from Saagwalla as possible. If Lily had been conscious, she would have barely recognized the Chia Man. His green hair had grown into a huge mossy halo, maybe two feet in diameter. His face didn't look like regular skin anymore.

"His skin has become barky, and he has little horns sprouting from his head that look kind of like antlers . . . no, actually they're more like beginning branches. His lips and eyes are rounder, like the knots in a tree." The Rose stopped abruptly, realizing what it was saying.

"Oh," Lily gasped, "he's becoming a tree! He's one of

Saagwalla's experiments." They were pondering his fate when something shocking happened.

"I can hear every word you're saying," a voice intruded into their thoughts. The Silver Rose and Lily instantly stopped chatting.

"I didn't mean to eavesdrop, it just sort of happened," the voice continued. "I know you're talking about me."

The Rose saw that Chia Man was staring at Lily as Saagwalla hovered over her attaching some electrodes to her head.

"It's the Chia Man," thought the Rose to Lily. "He's communicating like a plant!"

Lily and the Rose were both startled. Lily was full of a million questions, particularly because she was a botanist and had never encountered such a man/plant phenomenon before.

"Who are you?" asked Lily.

"My name is Albert Wedgie. But I don't know *what* I am anymore," said the voice sadly.

"Where did you come from? How did you get like this?"

"I was an environmentalist; a member of Trees Pleese. I went door to door, urging people to sign a petition encouraging the planting of more trees for a cleaner, greener world."

"I know that organization," said Lily. "Very commendable work."

"Thank you. One day I called on the home of Henry Saagwalla. I should have known better. Everyone knows his reputation. His house was devoid of any greenery. For one whole mile surrounding it there was nothing but gray cement. When I rang

157

the bell, Henry Saagwalla answered the door. I very politely told him about my petition, and I asked him to sign. If looks could kill, his would have. He invited me in for tea. Next thing I know, I wake up months later with green hair."

"But you work for the Hubrises!" said Lily.

"I can't help it. Every day Luella the Horror forces me to take a drug. It makes me do whatever they tell me to, whether I want to or not. 'Drive the taxi! Cook the dinner! Chase the botanist! Navigate the yacht! Make the perfect martini!' It's horrible. I mean, I was never very much of an individualist, but this is ridiculous."

"Did they ask you to communicate with us?" asked Lily.

"No." Albert paused thoughtfully. "They didn't."

"That means you must be developing a will of your own despite the drugs."

"That's interesting, because I never really had much of a will of my own." Albert thought about this. "But how can I have a free will when Luella is still drugging me?"

Lily felt terrible about what she had to say next.

"When she started giving you drugs, my bet is you were mostly human with a little bit of plant. I'm sorry to say this, but judging from the Silver Rose's description of you, you're becoming more plant than human. If Saagwalla's serum was meant to turn you into a plant, and Luella's drugs were meant for use on a human . . . then the more planty you become, the less her drugs take effect." Albert gasped. He looked at his arm and noticed that his skin *was* becoming rough and somewhat barky.

"My name is Lily Verdant," added Lily. "I'm a botanist. I

have many friends in the sciences who are doctors. I bet I know someone who could reverse this process."

"I know who you are. You're a botanist above botanists," Chia Man gasped. "And the only thing Saagwalla talks about."

"I need you to help us escape."

"I'd love to, but how can *I* help you escape? I'm having a hard time getting about myself. My joints are stiff, I can barely lift my arms, and you are, if you don't mind me saying so, dead weight. Someone's definitely going to notice me wheeling a gurney, the Silver Rose, and an intravenous feeding device out of the cave."

"You can do anything you put your mind to," thought Lily. "We need to formulate a plan."

A sound erupted from Albert that seemed like a *harrumph*.

Claude Hubris was so startled by the sound of the *harrumph* that he spilled a drop of his blue martini on his white linen suit, which upset him greatly. Henry Saagwalla had just finished detaching a couple of electrodes. He turned in Albert's direction.

"What was that sound?" Claude Hubris asked Henry Saagwalla.

Albert strained to hear the two men.

"The Chia Man. It's only a matter of time before he grows roots. He won't be able to move—then he'll die in here. No sunlight. Those irritating noises are just the last vestiges of his speech. He must be very happy, though." Saagwalla smiled sarcastically. "After all, he loved trees so much, and now he gets to be one!"

Albert was horrified. Lily sensed his anguish.

"Albert! Albert Wedgie! Listen to me!"

"I *am* becoming a tree," wailed Albert, almost hysterical.

"Then we've got to think fast, don't we?" Lily took a deep breath. "There's something I need to know, Albert . . . what does Henry Saagwalla want with me?" There was a long silence.

"I don't know exactly . . . but I do know that they're after someone else who they said is special, just like you."

Lily was confused. This couldn't be true? There was no one else "special like her" . . . except . . . was it possible that Henry Saagwalla was after Fern?

"I've got to get out of here as soon as possible!" Lily was very worried indeed.

Fern Takes Action

Fern was in a little cabin below the deck of the *Barracuda*. It was the size of a closet. There was no porthole. In it was a tiny bunk, a micro-closet, and a bathroom the size of your thumb. The door was locked from the outside, and her fellow prisoner, the Silver Petal, was placed on a small table beside the bed. Fern was grateful for the company. They talked; the Petal telepathically, Fern in whispers.

"What now?" asked the Petal.

"I don't know! But I must get back to the *Porpoise*."

Outside the door, Oren stood sentry. Dr. Marita Von Svenson passed by occasionally, her icy voice slicing through the ocean air.

"Oren, stand straighter. Suck in your stomach! A sloppy posture means a sloppy mind."

Fern wondered where they were going and why. She asked the Petal, but it had no idea. Fern was frustrated that she still had to talk with her mouth, and hoped this telepathy thing would kick in soon.

She took stock of her prison. In the small bathroom was a minuscule sink and shower. She never knew why people used the expression "it was so small you couldn't swing a cat." Now she knew. This bathroom was so small you couldn't swing a mouse. She peered into the sink and down the drain. Perhaps Fern could push the Petal down it, and the Petal could wriggle out and find help. The Petal reminded Fern that flexibility was an issue, not to mention the potential for rust. Fern knocked on the walls of the cabin; perhaps she could break her way out somehow, but the walls were all quite solid. She flopped on the mini-bunk, millions of thoughts running through her head. She hoped the orphans had been able to fix the *Porpoise* and weren't just bobbing in the middle of the ocean on a burned-out boat under the hot sun.

Through the door, Fern heard Oren the guard burp loudly. *Gross,* thought Fern. Where on earth did Marita find these lunkheads? She heard Oren burp again. That burp was like a bell going off in her head. If anyone was going to help her off this boat, it certainly wouldn't be Dr. Marita Von Svenson. Who was left?

"Oren? Oren the guard? Are you there?" Fern called.

"Shut up." Oren burped as if to punctuate his command.

"Did you know that in some countries burping is considered a sign of extreme intelligence?" Fern said.

There was a thoughtful silence on the other side of the door. Oren had been called many things in his life, but never "intelligent."

"What countries?"

Fern thought back to the maps in her atlas.

"Um, China, Madagascar, and Uruguay."

"China, Mada-mada-mada-agascar, and Uruguay?" Oren repeated, making a mental note that when this job was over he must take a vacation in these three countries.

"Yes. As well as several others whose names escape me right now. It's a little hot in here, and hard for me to think," Fern said.

"Then maybe you should just be quiet."

"How did Dr. Marita Von Svenson manage to get a smart henchthug like you to work for her? She must be paying you buckets of money."

"I said, shut up!" Oren barked.

"I could certainly use someone like you right now."

Silence.

"Where does a person find quality bodyguards like yourself?"

"*Criminals Weekly.* She placed a general ad. 'Henchthugs wanted. Travel and adventure. Good career opportunities.' "

"How much do you get paid?" Fern paused. "It must be a lot since I appear to be very valuable. Why else chase me halfway around the world?"

There was an under-the-breath grumbling outside the door.

"You can tell me how much. I bet she's throwing in a trip to some far-off land with hula dancers and butterflies the size of kites."

"I said, SHUT UP!" Oren was losing his patience.

"I'm sorry." Fern seemed slightly embarrassed for him. "I just assumed . . ."

"Minimum wage and expenses," Oren mumbled.

"You're worth so much more than that." Fern gave a sympathetic sigh. Then, "Oh, I get it . . . I know what she did!"

"What? What?" asked Oren, anxious to know why someone as brilliant as himself could be working for so little.

"She hypnotized you," said Fern. "Hypnotism is her specialty."

There was dead quiet again on the other side of the door. Fern pressed her ear against it. She heard the clumping approach of another pair of heavy boots and then whispering.

"Um, Igor, um . . . have we been hypnotized?" asked Oren.

"*Nyet,*" Igor answered.

"Go get Blood," Fern heard Oren say. A couple of minutes later another big heavy set of boots came clumping down the hall.

"Blood, why aren't we getting a lot of money for this job?"

Fern heard Blood choke with laughter.

"You read the ad—minimum and expenses."

"It doesn't seem right. Do you think it's possible we may have been hypnotized?" Oren asked.

"Naaa," said Igor. If Fern had been on the other side of the door, she would have seen Igor staring intently into the eyes of Oren and Blood.

"How do you know?" asked Oren.

"It's in the eyes. In my old country many unhappy people hypnotized by government so would not know they were unhappy. I have seen it."

"So, then, why are we out here getting ordered around by that crazy lady?" asked Oren. "I don't feel like I'm having an adventure, and I'm not getting rich." Fern heard more silence. "And the food is disgusting." They all looked at each other, feeling stupid.

Fern whispered through the door. "What if I paid you to help rescue me?"

She could hear three deep voices mumbling and conferring.

"How much?" asked Oren.

"A lot," bluffed Fern. "I know where the rest of the Silver Rose is. It's extremely valuable; the only one of its kind in the whole world." The Silver Petal protested. Fern shushed it. She could hear the three guards mumbling and whispering.

"That's mutiny. It could give us bad names as henchthugs. We'd be unemployable," said Oren.

"But we'd be rich. Maybe rich enough to retire," said Blood.

"Ya . . . maybe never have to work as henchthugs again," added Igor.

"No more being the bad guy," Oren said.

"Okay," said Blood, Oren, and Igor together. Fern heard the locks unlock. She put the Petal in her pocket and stepped outside to find her three employees waiting for orders.

"There better be a lot of money in that stinking Rose, because we're putting our careers on the line here."

Fern was a little nervous. She'd never had her own hench-thugs before, and of course she was completely bluffing about payment.

"Right. The first thing we've got to do is take over this boat, then go find the *Porpoise*. Okay?"

"Okay," they responded.

"We need to get that Vapor-icer off of Dr. Marita Von Sven-son, otherwise she could freeze us all and smash us to bits. Where does she keep it?"

"In a holster," said Blood.

The doctor was on the deck of the *Barracuda*, multitasking. She had one eye on another henchthug, Dirk, as he piloted the boat, while she rifled through Fern's backpack looking for any-thing of interest. She was also on a walkie-talkie.

Oren, Blood, and Igor crept up behind her, followed by Fern. Marita couldn't hear them approach because she was shout-ing into the walkie-talkie in order to be heard over the wind and the waves. Fern strained to hear Marita's conversation, hoping for some clue that would tell her why she was on board this boat. Gusts of wind carried words past Fern. She heard, "prisoner" and "gift," but the rest of the words were lost in the wind until three very clear words floated past. They were "yes, Mr. Saagwalla."

Fern cringed. Had she heard correctly? Could Marita Von Svenson possibly be talking to the man behind her mother's kidnapping? Then, as if to respond to Fern's unspoken question, Dr. Marita Von Svenson said, "Of course, Mr. Saagwalla." She got off the walkie-talkie and turned her attention back to Fern's scattered belongings. When she looked up, she saw three of her henchthugs standing awkwardly in front of her. Fern was hidden behind them. Oren stepped up nervously. He was designated spokes-thug.

"We're officially taking over this v-v-vessel," stammered Oren with no authority in his voice whatsoever. With that, Oren picked Marita up by the scruff of her neck, like a Swedish kitten. Dirk stared with his mouth open. Marita reached for her Vapor-icer, but Fern was too quick. She scooped the weapon out of Marita's hand before the psychiatrist had a chance to freeze anyone.

"You ridiculous freak of nature!" Marita was dangerously close to raising her voice. "Put me down! Now!"

Fern leveled the Vapor-icer at Marita.

"You can't keep me prisoner anymore! I don't care who you're working for!" Then Fern remembered her partners in crime. "And you cannot go on treating these noble henchthugs like slaves." Oren, Igor, Blood, and even Dirk were all overcome by emotion. No one had ever stood up for them before. Fern returned her belongings to her backpack and slung it over her shoulder. She stared Dr. Marita Von Svenson right in the eyes.

"You will not keep me from finding my mother!" she announced.

Then Dr. Marita Von Svenson did the last thing that Fern ever thought she would do in this situation: she chuckled. It was the first time Fern had seen her come close to a laugh. It was a small laugh, more like seeing a hairline crack in a frozen pond. You had to look closely to find it, but the sound she uttered was definitely a chuckle. Fern was confused by the response.

"You stupid little twit . . . I'm not going to prevent you from finding your mother. In fact, that's exactly where I am taking you."

Everyone looked at everyone else, confused. Fern leveled the Vapor-icer at Marita.

"That's perfect then, isn't it?" Fern was trying to cover her confusion. "But now, you'll be *my* prisoner. First we're going to make sure Anthony and Francesca and the others are all fine."

"Whatever you say." Marita's voice had become soothing and melodic. "You're the captain now. I will follow you now. I repeat, I will follow you, even if you are sleepy. You must all be sleepy . . . so very sleepy . . . such a long day." Oren was still holding Marita in the air. She stared deeply into his eyes. His knees began to wobble.

Blood and Igor were listening intently to Marita. Her voice had become like a river that they desperately wanted to swim in. Their eyes were getting droopy. Fern realized what was happening and averted her gaze.

"Look away!" she cried to the henchthugs. It was too late. The henchthugs were not strong of mind, and their brains buckled in seconds. Even Fern felt strange and weak, and Marita had only gazed into her eyes for the briefest of moments. Fern held on to the side of the boat for support. She tried to lift the Vapor-icer and take aim, but it felt heavy in her hand.

"Very sleepy, very sleepy, very sleepy," repeated Marita. Even Dirk was beginning to nod off at the helm of the boat.

Fern shook her head to rid herself of the dozy feeling that was overcoming her. Oren dropped Marita back onto the deck.

"Listen to me, obey me, listen to me, obey me," Marita's hypnotic voice took on a singsong quality. She started walking toward Fern. Fern looked away. Marita was getting closer and closer. Fern backed into the side of the boat. There was only one avenue of escape that presented itself to Fern. Plugging her nose, Vapor-icer in hand, backpack over her shoulder, and Petal in her pocket, Fern let herself fall backward over the side of the *Barracuda*, like a scuba diver, splashing into the enormous blue Pacific Ocean.

Overboard

When Fern looked up from beneath the waves, she saw a huddle of blurry faces leaning over the side of the *Barracuda*. The glazed expressions of Oren, Blood, and Igor looked dimly down at the face of their former prisoner/leader. Dr. Von Svenson's emotionless face was frozen, staring at Fern, who sank, weighted by the bulk of her backpack. Fern saw Oren disappear. When he reappeared, he was holding a long pole with a net at the end. He thrashed it about in the water, trying to reach Fern, but she was just beyond the net's reach.

Fern jammed the Vapor-icer in her backpack to free up her hand, and started swimming downward, away from the *Barracuda*, away from air, away from life, and toward the beds of seaweed that undulated in the water beneath her. Fern had read enough in her mother's books to know that if she could see a forest of seaweed below her, then she might be in fairly shallow water. And fairly shallow water could mean land nearby.

While it might seem a foolish thing to plunge headfirst into an ocean without scuba equipment or a life jacket, Fern felt she had no other choice. Dr. Von Svenson was trying to hypnotize her, and one single question could erase Fern's gift. Many thoughts flashed through her head, *I have to get to my mother, I have to get to the* Porpoise, *I have to find out if the orphans are safe, I need to see my father and Grandmamma Lisette again*, but there was one surprising thought that came from some deep, instinctive place inside her. It was *I must preserve my gift*. The feeling was so intense that she knew she had to heed it. She held her breath and swam down, down toward the seaweed. She wished she were a mermaid so she could just swim to the *Porpoise*. In her pocket the metal Petal was expressing serious concerns.

"Swim up to the air!" the Petal thought to Fern. "Or you'll die!" Fern ignored the warning. She dove deeper and deeper.

"Seaweed! I am the daughter of Lily Verdant!" she gurgled.

Blue, yellow, red, and pink fish zigzagged in front of Fern. A big manta ray wafted within inches of her face. It looked at her, its odd beady eyes poking out of its flat, wavy form, then drifted off into the deep. Free-floating tubular strands of seaweed danced like seahorses. The shadow of the *Barracuda* floated ominously above her. Fern focused like she had never focused before, crying out for help to the myriad species of seaweed inhabiting the ocean around her, asking any one of them, anywhere, to please help the daughter of Lily Verdant.

Fern felt weak and cold. Everything started to grow hazy.

Strange things floated in the water. Just in front of her she saw a blurry vision, a giant, mustard-colored seaweed blob, like some strange kind of submarine. It was the last thing Fern remembered before fading into blackness.

When Fern finally opened her eyes again, there was nothing but darkness. She felt very, very hot. She coughed, spitting up sea water. Fern realized she must be dead. She screamed, surprised that a person could actually scream when they were dead. When she sat up, a thick slab of slimy seaweed slid off her face and fell to the ground with a plop. The slab had blocked out the bright sunlight. Fern squinted.

"Ewww!" she said to herself, wiping some slime off her face with the back of her hand. The Slab lay on the hot sand like a black lump of jelly. It had heart-shaped markings on it, but aside from that, it was pretty ugly. Fern looked down at the stuff, and thought, *Gross . . . I can't believe that thing was on my face.*

"I heard that," announced the Slab.

These conversations still startled Fern. She turned red. "Sorry. I didn't mean . . ."

"You're an ingrate! I was lying on your face so you wouldn't get burned," it said, indignant. "You were unconscious forever, you big log! I was only protecting you from the sun. Now you can kindly put me back in the water, thank you very much. I'm shriveling up out here."

"I . . . I didn't mean to insult you. It's just that waking up in a strange place with slime on your face . . . it's disconcerting. I'm sorry."

Fern looked around, discombobulated. She felt crusty. Her

hair was a tangle of black curls, sand, and sea salt. She was sitting on a beautiful sandy shoreline that disappeared in an arc of beach in both directions. She was just a few feet from the water. Palm trees swayed behind her in the gentle wafting breeze. There were no houses or people. She reached into her pocket and found, to her great relief, the Petal. She was quite attached to it by now. The Petal was the only one who knew precisely what she'd been through.

"You okay?" she asked the Petal.

"You might want to dry me off," it replied. "I'm feeling rusty."

"Where am I?" asked Fern, dazed.

"You're on an island," said the Slab, stating the obvious. "You were rescued in a seaweed sub, and transported away from that boat. You were resurfaced and brought to the nearest island. They ordered me to protect your face from frying."

"They?" asked Fern.

The Slab sluggishly shifted its malleable black bulk into an arrow and pointed out to sea. Fern saw hundreds of tubular seaweed heads sticking out of the water like eels, slimy and shaking and shimmering in the sun, necks craned anxiously toward the shore. Fern looked gratefully out to her slippery audience.

"I need water!" rasped the Slab, making a mock choking sound. "The tide receded and now I'm stuck." Fern got up on wobbly legs.

She stooped down and picked up the seaweed. The heart-shaped markings on its back, or front, or whatever it was she was looking at, were quite pretty . . . they looked turquoise in the sun. "You know, those are very pretty markings you have." Fern wanted to make amends for her rudeness.

"Ahhhhh!" the Slab wailed. "Did you have to point out my horrid birthmark? You're too cruel."

Fern said nothing. She was afraid to speak for fear of offending the Slab yet again. She walked to the water's edge and floated the Slab in the surf. It slithered out to sea.

"Thank you so much for your help!" Fern watched the blob disappear into the waves.

The periscopes of seaweed bent a little as though they were bowing to her, and disappeared below the surface. Fern sat back on her heels for a moment, getting her bearings. Her backpack lay nearby. It had completely dried out in the tropical sun.

"Any idea where we are?" Fern asked the Petal.

"Looks like an island to me." Fern was just about to say something smart in response, when the Petal let out a gasp.

"What?"

"Look at you!" it exclaimed. "Don't you realize what's happened? Your lips aren't moving! You're speaking telepathically . . . you've been speaking telepathically since you washed up on shore!" Recent events had been such that Fern hadn't really had time to notice she wasn't speaking with her mouth.

"At last! How strange and wonderful it feels to be able to think my thoughts to you instead of speaking." Then, in the distance, Fern noticed something glinting in the water—it was the *Barracuda*. She dropped to the sand and lay on her belly, watching as the *Barracuda* sped away from the island. The boat disappeared on the horizon. Dr. Marita Von Svenson must believe that Fern had drowned.

"We've got to figure out how to get off this island." Fern slipped the Petal into her pocket, and set off to explore. She walked along the shoreline and then turned inland toward a small hill and a patch of palm trees. When she crested the incline, she realized the landmass couldn't be more than a square mile in size. There were lots of palm trees, a few banana trees, and little else. Fern decided to have a talk with one of the locals. She was quite proud of her newfound skill, and she couldn't wait to try it out.

The palms were clustered in a little group. Coconuts swayed in the air above her head, bunched beneath the very high fronds. Fern picked the tallest palm, assuming it might be the oldest and the wisest.

"Hello, Palm," Fern said telepathically.

The Palm was surprised to have a human talk with it. It had heard rumors of conversations betweens trees and humans, but had never actually participated in one. Out here in the middle of the Pacific Ocean, there wasn't much foot traffic.

"Hey, man," said the Palm. "Wellllcome to our islaaand."

The Palm spoke slowly, like it was speaking to an idiot.

"You don't have to talk like that," said Fern, "and I'm not a man. I'm a girl."

"Oh," said the Palm. "Whatever . . . can I help you?"

"I'm looking for food and water. And a way off this island?"

Fern heard a rustling sound. A rain of coconuts and bananas

fell at her feet. She backed away to avoid being bonked on the head.

"That's the good news. You can drink the coconut milk and eat the bananas."

"What's the bad news?" asked Fern.

"Well, man . . . I mean, girl," said the Palm, "there is no way off this island, unless you have a boat. The last time we had a human stranded here . . ." The Tallest Palm paused. "Well, it totally did not have a happy ending."

"What happened?"

"I was just a sapling at the time, barely a twig. This was years ago. Poor guy didn't have a very good time of it. He ran round like a crazy thing. Lived in that shack . . ." The Palm pointed with its fronds. Fern saw the remnants of a lean-to built against a couple of trees.

"He ate nothing but coconuts and bananas for years. One day he started acting very strangely, hitting himself on the head with coconuts, and then he fell to the ground wailing. Later, he just totally ran out into the surf, flailing his arms, and disappeared under the water . . . never came back. You really gotta chill here, man . . . um, girl. Enjoy the sea and the sky. Don't worry about leaving. Life is beautiful. Be happy." The Palm swayed back and forth in the tropical breeze.

As far as Fern was concerned life was not beautiful. She wasn't feeling very confident at the moment, and it was apparent she'd get no helpful advice from the Palm. One bonus of being the offspring of botanists was the amount of time you were forced to spend outdoors. She had gone camping with

Olivier and Lily many times when she was little. She knew that once night fell it would be chilly, and she also knew she needed to attract passing boats or planes to the island . . . she had to be rescued one way or the other.

Fern gathered up some dead leaves and twigs. Then, after apologizing to it profusely, she used the more metal part of the Petal to magnify the sun's rays and start a fire on the beach. She watched hopefully as the smoke from the blaze spiraled up, but it seemed that there was no one out here to see it. The sun went down, and it did get chilly. Fern and the Petal huddled by the fire. Fern lay down, holding the Petal in her hand, her head resting on her backpack. The waves brushed against the tiny pebbles of the shoreline. They tumbled about, sounding like crab claws clacking. Fern thought about her mother. She thought about how many adventures just like this one her mother must have had all around the world. She wished more than anything that they had been able to talk about them, so that she had some inkling of what to do in a pickle such as this.

Castaway

The next morning when Fern woke up, she forgot where she was for a moment. Then the warm water of the Pacific lapped up on the shoreline over her toes, and she remembered. She ate coconut and banana for breakfast, and considered her options. There were only two ways to get off this island: hope to be rescued by someone else, or escape on her own. The first way required sitting around and waiting until goodness knows when. The second way seemed more proactive. Fern gave it some thought, then stood up, brushed the sand from her lap, set the Petal in her backpack, and walked determinedly out into the sea. As the water reached her hips, she dove under the waves and swam.

The Tallest Palm watched from its elevated vantage point and thought, *Good grief . . . that one certainly didn't last long.* But this girl was very different from that other human. Fern had an inquiry to make, and she thought it was only polite to make it face to weed. She swam out to a patch of particularly robust seaweed.

"I hate to be demanding," she said telepathically, "but I need to borrow the Mustard Submarine Weed to get to the *Porpoise*. It's a bright orange fishing boat floating out in the ocean." The seaweed was very aware of the *Porpoise*'s location, and pointed out the direction to Fern, but the Mustard Submarine would be useless, it said. That particular bulbous bloat of seaweed did not hold enough oxygen for Fern to travel as far as the *Porpoise*. The Seaweed said that the *Porpoise* had drifted far out to sea. Fern swam back to shore. She dried off in the sun and considered her second option . . . building a raft.

Fern knew she had to approach this matter very delicately— after all, what could one make a raft out of but wood. It felt wrong to chop down something you could have a conversation with. Fern approached the Tallest Palm.

"Is there anything on this island I could build a raft from?" she asked. The Tallest Palm thought about it.

"Well, I had an uncle who was blown over in a hurricane once." The Palm paused for a moment, upset. "Ripped his roots right out of the ground. That was by the water's edge. You could have made a raft out of him. But he's gone, washed out to sea." The Tallest Palm fell silent. Fern didn't know what to do. She was tired and completely at a loss. She sat at the base of the tree, and started crying.

"Hey, chill," said the Palm. "Nothing can be that bad."

"My mother is Lily Verdant, the only other person in the whole world who can talk to plants. She has been kidnapped by a crazy, evil gazillionaire who made his money destroying nature, and right now she's in a coma. I don't know where she is, except it's somewhere far away. Oh, and I might have accidentally killed a boat full of orphans."

The Tallest Palm was very quiet. It hadn't expected this long list of troubles!

"If I don't get to the *Porpoise*, and if my mother doesn't get saved, then there will be no one left in the whole world who can hear the calls of dying species," Fern added, crying in the sand. The Palm could feel the tears falling on its roots. This was the last straw.

"That is bad!" The Palm joined in the sobbing, sap rolling down his length. "I've never heard such a woeful story in my life, but then I haven't heard that many stories, period." Fern felt the sticky, sappy tears accumulating at her feet.

"Take me!" cried the Palm. "Take me! I've had a long life. I want to do something good. Chop me down. Build a raft! Save the world!"

Fern looked up at the Palm, quite touched by the offer.

"I couldn't do that. For one thing I don't have an ax. For another, I couldn't chop down a tree I've just had a conversation with . . . or any tree for that matter. But it's very kind of you to offer." Fern got up and patted the Palm's bark. "There must be another way." She turned her attention back to the sea. Fern could feel herself getting sunburned, so she reached into her pack to pull out a long-sleeved shirt and a cap. When she did, her hand bumped against something metal in the bottom of the pack. It was Dr. Marita Von Svenson's Vapor-icer. Fern had completely forgotten about it in the chaos of the last twenty-four hours.

She pulled it from her backpack. Water dribbled out of it. There hadn't been much time to examine the weapon when she seized it from the doctor. It had four dials. One dial read *depth*, a second dial read *length*, a third dial read *width*, and a fourth very creepy dial read *targets*. Under *targets* were the words *animal/man*, *plant*, and *other*. Fern shuddered. She knew that if you froze a person or an animal or a flower they would die. Below the *target* dial was a timer. It started at *thirty seconds* and finished at *permanent*. Fern had an idea.

"That's brilliant!" interrupted the Petal, reading Fern's thoughts.

"It is, isn't it?" She stuffed her belongings back in her pack and headed to the water's edge. Then she had a horrible thought. Looking out over the ocean, she knew there were many living plants and fish in that water. In fact, the very seaweed that had rescued her was somewhere out there. What if it was caught in the ice? The ice would kill anything in its path. It could be frozen solid. Fern did not want to be responsible for the end of any living creature. She was becoming quite sensitive about these things.

"Send out an All Plants Bulletin," said the Petal.

"I don't know if I can." Fern had never sent one out all by herself.

She was torn. She needed to use the Vapor-icer to escape,

but if she failed to successfully send out an APB, the seaweed and everything else caught in the icy path would die. Even worse, if she didn't use the ice gun, then her mother and many, many other plants might perish.

"You have to," urged the Petal.

Fern was nervous. "I know."

Fern closed her eyes and concentrated. With all of the focus she could gather, she sent out a message. It said, "For your own safety, please stay away from the water's surface, and please, if you can, tell the fish to do the same." She opened her eyes. The ocean looked exactly the same. There was no way of knowing if the message had been received.

Fern sighed, and set the *depth* dial on the Vapor-icer for six inches. She raised the weapon, pointed it at the water, and fired. A stream of vapor flew from the barrel of the gun and tumbled along the ocean surface.

The thick vapor solidified on the water into an ice path, six inches deep and four feet wide. It inched right up onto the sand where the waves ended. But there was a problem. It was only five feet long. Five feet of ice was not going to bring Fern anywhere near the *Porpoise*. Fern looked down at the *length* dial. She had set it for *As Far as the Eye Can See*, and thought that it would be sufficient. Fern shook the Vapor-icer. Something rattled inside. More water dribbled out of it. Perhaps it was broken. Fern aimed the weapon again. More vapor appeared, but only another five feet. Water splashed over the sides of the second five feet of ice.

"Well, five feet *is* five feet," Fern said to herself. She would just have to walk out to the *Porpoise* five feet at a time. She strapped her pack on her back, made sure the Petal was safe in her pocket, and was about to step on the icy path when she remembered something. She ran back to the Tallest Palm.

"Thank you for your kindness." Fern hugged its trunk.

"Be safe." The Tallest Palm sniffled. "I know you're going to do great things."

Fern returned to the water's edge. The ice floated out in front of her on the surface of the warm Pacific. Fern took a big breath and stepped out onto the frosty surface.

"Aahhh," she screamed, and jumped back onto the warm sand. Fern had been barefoot since swimming into the sea at Dollop. Walking on ice with no shoes was a bad idea. She dug around in her backpack and pulled out her hiking boots, then stepped once more onto the icy path. Much better. Carefully placing one foot in front of the other, Fern headed out onto the surface of the ocean, where she hoped to find the stranded *Porpoise*.

Fern fired the Vapor-icer, creating five-foot lengths of ice, intending to keep thirty or forty feet of visible path ahead of her. She was feeling proud of this plan, until she was about sixty feet out onto the water. Turning around for a cursory glance to shore, she saw that the first forty feet of her ice path had melted . . . completely. Fern stood on a length of twenty feet of ice, the first ten feet of which were beginning to melt, unsure of her next step. It was obvious the Vapor-icer was malfunctioning. What should she do? Take a chance, and continue on out to where she hoped to find the *Porpoise*, or retreat to the safety of the shore while she still could? But when she thought of the crazy castaway who'd fled into the ocean and certain death, Fern knew she couldn't just hang around, waiting to get saved. She had to continue on. She raised the Vapor-icer and created another five feet.

The ice was clear, and Fern could see beneath her into the sea. Thousands of fish—big and small, benign and threatening—lined up below to watch Fern as she made her way out on the surface of the sea. Most of these creatures had never seen ice; after all, they lived in the balmy Pacific. It was strange and wonderful. Little fins reached up to curiously brush against the transparent surface, and then shrank back from the icy cold. Fern felt as though she was on a stage performing for a fishy audience. Dolphins leapt out of the water on one side of the path, floating over Fern's head and pirouetting back into the sea on the other side of the ice. Fern was amazed at the beauty of it all.

Beneath her, a smallish gray shark nudged at the ice, irritated that this transparent barrier was keeping him away from what could be a perfect meal. Although Fern knew nothing about sharks, this one was only about three feet in length and seemed to be young. Occasionally its head would break the surface of the water. All the other fish fled, looking like prisms of colorful scattering glass. The shark's teeth glistened in the sun before the creature dove below the surface again and swam beneath the path. It was very unnerving. Fern stopped in her tracks, looking right down into the shark's eyes. Only six inches of ice separated them. The shark looked at Fern.

"Shooo!" cried Fern, immediately realizing the silliness of

the command. An annoyed expression crossed the shark's eyes, as though it had just been insulted. It quickly turned away and disappeared below the surface with a swish of its tail.

Fern skidded here and there when waves lapped especially far over the path, making it extra-slippery. Every few feet she shot the ice gun. Glancing back, she watched the path disappear behind her. Beyond that, the island receded in size, becoming a little bump in the horizon, with the tall stalks of the palm trees barely visible. Fern turned her attention ahead, anxious to see the bright orange of the *Porpoise*. She was so focused on the horizon that it took her completely by surprise when something enormous hit the ice path from below, sending Fern several feet into the air before she landed on her bottom, spinning in circles on the ice. On close inspection Fern could see the ice was cracked.

She scrambled to all fours, and was just about to stand up when she saw a dark gray, twelve-foot-long shark bearing quickly up from below.

"Aggggggghhhhhh!" Fern screamed as the shark's snout butted the bottom of the ice path again. She flew up into the air, and then spiraled back down onto the increasingly cracked path. The shark disappeared below, preparing for another attack. In a flash Fern aimed the ice gun. She pulled the trigger and scrambled onward. The shark rammed the spot she'd just left, and was quite shocked to find no Fern staring down through the ice. It glanced around and spied the fresh path, then swam away, down into the depths, in order to gain momentum. Fern pulled the trigger of the ice gun, and created more path.

"Run! Run!" the Petal screamed in Fern's head.

"Excuse me, but what do you think I'm doing?" Fern shrieked back.

As Fern forged ahead, she noticed something black and round in the path in front of her. She skidded to a stop, and to her horror, she saw the frozen form of the Slab embedded in the ice. "Oh, no!" she cried. The Slab's distinctive heart-shaped marks were visible through the ice. It was gray and inert.

"Oh . . . I'm so sorry." But the Slab could not hear her. It was dead. Fern felt horrible—her APB had been a miserable failure. When she looked closely, she saw bits and pieces of lifeless, frozen seaweed entombed all around her. Suddenly the shark appeared below her again, zooming upward for another attack. Fern scrambled ahead, zigzagging the path to confuse the beast. Left, then right, then left, the path veered. The shark was slowing down; the constant pounding on its snout was taking a toll. The smaller shark appeared by its side.

Fern was fairly far out at sea now, and the island was barely visible. As she skittered and slid across the ice, she thought she saw something in the distance, something orange. The shark had given up head-butting the path and had resorted to plan B: rising up out of the sea, jaws wide, trying to snap up Fern. Fern clung to the ice, avoiding the beast by crawling as fast and low as she could on her belly. A particularly big wave ebbed in front of her and revealed in the distance a flash of orange against the blue sea. Faster and faster she crawled, firing the Vapor-icer as quickly as she could, the shark now furious.

Anthony was standing on the burned and crusty deck of the

boat, binoculars to his eyes, when he saw the most extraordinary thing he'd ever seen. Out in the water, Fern Verdant was scrambling along on her belly on a path made of ice, while a mammoth shark snapped and strained and struggled to get at her. She was waving her hands and screaming at the top of her lungs. This girl certainly had spunk.

Land Ahoy

The *Porpoise* had been pretty badly damaged, and it was a mess. Anthony was still trying to fix the engine, when he spied Fern. The ice path ended abruptly just a foot from the *Porpoise*. Anthony leaned out to grab Fern, but at that moment the shark burst out of the water between them, sending Fern flying back onto the ice and Anthony back onto the boat. As the shark disappeared into the ocean to prepare for the next attack, Anthony reached out again and grabbed Fern's hand. He hoisted her onboard. Fern collapsed on deck, more relieved than she had ever been in her life. The shark spiraled into the air and took a last look at the girl before gliding, frustrated and exhausted, back into the Pacific, followed by his even more frustrated smaller friend.

"It's beautiful!" Francesca looked in amazement at the ice

path as it melted and mingled with the ocean water. A few fish tried to take souvenirs, unaware of the futility of keeping a sliver of ice as a keepsake.

"Marita Von Svenson's Vapor-icer." Fern held it up.

"How long was that shark chasing you?" Anthony asked, trying to keep the hint of admiration out of his voice.

"I don't know," said Fern. "It felt like forever."

"Wow!" Kai reached out for the peculiar weapon, but Fern tucked it away in her pack.

"I'm sure it'll come in handy, but it's very dangerous." She thought of the poor Slab that had met its end in the ice.

Jane, Tim, and Lulu hung back, still unsure about Fern.

"I'm sorry about the tracking device!" said Fern. "I would never have intentionally led anyone to you in a million years."

"It doesn't matter if you meant to, you still led them to us!" Kai looked at her accusingly, doubly annoyed because she hadn't let him play with the Vapor-icer.

"Don't worry about it," said Anthony. Everyone gawked at him, shocked to hear these words come out of his mouth. But Anthony was smart. He knew that if Fern had packed the tracking device intentionally, she never would have risked her life to return to the *Porpoise*. He also remembered the strange funnel of water whipped up by the seaweed Fern had spoken with. He was beginning to forget that he should mistrust her because she wasn't an orphan, and instead was intrigued by this increasingly mysterious girl.

"I know you think the Petal is a way for you to never be poor again," Fern pulled the Silver Petal out of her pocket. "But I think there must be other ways." Fern pressed the Petal into Anthony's palm. "As a show of trust, keep this until we find my mother." The Petal protested, but Fern said it was the right thing to do, that this way they would all be a team. Fern told the orphans about the deserted island, and how Dr. Marita Von Svenson must believe that Fern was dead and that the *Porpoise* was destroyed. She told them that the psychiatrist was in league with a man named Henry Saagwalla, who hated nature. With the Vapor-icer in their possession, Fern believed that nothing would be able to harm them as they searched for her mother.

"Why did he kidnap her?" asked Anthony. Fern paused. She hated to lie, but then she realized she didn't know exactly what horrible plan Saagwalla had in mind for her mother, so technically, it really wasn't a lie.

"I don't actually know why he's kidnapped her. But I do know that Henry Saagwalla is a very evil man and that if we don't find my mother, terrible things may happen in the world."

Anthony stared at her intently. "Okay," he said.

"There's just one problem. Our engine is smashed to bits. I'm trying to fix it, and I think I can, but even if I do, we only have the gas that's in the tank. We threw our last gas cans overboard so we wouldn't explode. We'll have to get more fuel from somewhere."

Fern thought about this. She thought about the coughing seaweed and about the ugly gas ruining the ocean. She had an idea.

"That gas ends up in this beautiful sea. It pollutes everything. It kills plants and fish. If there was a way for us to sail

190

without it, we wouldn't wreck the ocean. And we wouldn't have to go ashore and risk dealing with adults." Fern's life as a protector was officially beginning. "Besides, then the only thing we'd be dependent on is the wind."

That independence appealed to Anthony. "It's a good thing we're nowhere near the Doldrums." He constructed a makeshift mast out of wood they salvaged from below deck. He rigged it onto the boat. The entire crew helped sew together four tarpaulins that would function as a sail. Kai was very artistic, and on the tarpaulin sail he painted a beautiful picture of a large porpoise with six orphans laughing and clinging to its back. He didn't bother painting Fern on the porpoise because she wasn't an orphan and he was annoyed at her for more reasons than he could count. The *Porpoise* became an eco-friendly sailboat.

"Much better." Fern smiled as the wind billowed out the tarpaulins and the *Porpoise* continued its long voyage.

Now Fern and Francesca happily shared a bunk as roommates instead of guard and prisoner. Fern swabbed the deck and helped out in any way that she could. Everyone laughed when she imitated the expression on Dr. Marita Von Svenson's face as Fern jumped overboard from the *Barracuda*. With one exception, the other orphans became friendlier toward her.

"I still don't trust her," Kai said. "She's not an orphan."

"Oh, c'mon," Jane rasped. "I think you're being prejudiced toward her because she has parents."

"Besides," added Lulu, "if Anthony thinks it's safe to accept her . . ."

Tim had no opinion at all, because he generally had no opinion about anything other than navigation and maps.

Each morning Fern went up on deck and looked out to sea, waiting for the seaweed arrows to point toward her mother. She told Anthony which direction to turn, and she consulted Tim to see where these shifts in course were taking them. They passed islands, big and small. Sometimes, if the island was uninhabited, the *Porpoise* would anchor and the crew would row to shore in a little dinghy to stock up on fresh fruit and water, lingering to swim in sandy coves. They never stopped long. Everyone knew that time was of the essence in the search for Lily Verdant.

At night they all sat around a table in the galley and played games by lamplight. It was on these evenings that Fern heard the stories of the rest of the crew. The usually quiet Tim told his tale after supper one night.

"My mom left me with my grandmother when I was five. She never came back. When my grandmother died, I was put into a foster home. I was in ten foster homes in five years. In my last foster home, there was another kid."

"That was me!" piped in Lulu.

"We had both been there for a year when our foster mother got really sick. She couldn't care for us anymore, but I didn't want to be sent to another home. I met Anthony in town. He knew we were going to be sent away, and asked if we wanted to sail away on the *Porpoise* with him." Fern figured Tim must like maps because he'd moved around so much. Jane's story was equally sad. She'd been an orphan since a tragic accident when she was seven. Only Kai refused to share his history.

Over the next weeks they sailed past the Philippine Islands, through the South China Sea, past Borneo and Malaysia. Still the seaweed arrows pointed farther. The weather was hot and balmy. Sometimes tropical rains would deluge the *Porpoise*, and the orphans collected the rainwater in buckets. They saved it to drink.

The sun was warm, and the sky blue as they sailed across the splendid Indian Ocean. They had spent a great deal of time on deck, and when Fern looked in a mirror she was shocked to see a sun-kissed face staring back at her, framed by jet-black curls with odd blond streaks weaving through their length. Except for the blond streaks, it could have been a reflection of her mother.

They sailed like this for days. Early one morning Fern was on deck swabbing when she noticed something on the horizon. She picked up a pair of binoculars, and there in the distance she could make out the low-lying hills of a landform. Excited, Fern glanced over the side of the *Porpoise*. Below the water's surface were hundreds of thousands of lengths of seaweed. Each formed an arrow. Each arrow pointed toward the landmass. Fern dropped the binoculars and ran below deck, shouting, "We've found it!"

Within Reach

People often think that if they are not around, then nothing is happening because *they* are not there to experience it. That's not true. Fern was not in many places, but many things were still happening in those places.

One of those places was on board the *Barracuda*. Dr. Marita Von Svenson was now the captain of a crew of hypnotized henchthugs without a mission. The moment Fern fell overboard and "drowned," Marita knew her mission was ruined. Frightened of returning to Saagwalla without Fern, she thought it would be much better to be dead. So Dr. Marita Von Svenson hypnotized two of her henchthugs into believing that she was indeed dead. When she docked in Singapore, she sent them ashore.

The Singapore police found Dirk and Blood stumbling

around the streets, crying, "world-famous psychiatrist Dr. Marita Von Svenson eaten by giant squid." Since giant squid were very rare, the news made all the papers. In fact, Marita Von Svenson was still on the *Barracuda*. She had renamed it the *Guppy*. She painted the boat pink, dyed her blond hair brown, and lay on the deck tanning her pale skin. Her green eyes were turned blue with contact lenses that eliminated the need for glasses. Her business suits were traded in for sarongs. Marita Von Svenson was so pleased with her transformation that she didn't even notice the strange plane flying low over the *Guppy* in the Singapore harbor. She certainly didn't recognize the passenger of that plane, who was none other than Olivier Verdant.

Elsewhere, Henry Saagwalla was driven half crazy because he'd lost control of the situation. Since he was already half crazy . . . that meant he was now totally crazy. What to do with Lily Verdant? He had been very confident that Lily's talent had been passed on to her daughter. His suspicions were confirmed by his correspondence with his former undergraduate student, Dr. Marita Von Svenson. With mother and daughter held captive together, he knew he'd be able to extract any secrets he wanted. But things were not going his way. When Henry Saagwalla read about Dr. Marita Von Svenson's death, he was very upset, until he saw a TV interview with the two henchthugs. Dirk and Blood, their eyes looking vacant and distant, repeated the exact same words over and over. Saagwalla recognized the effects of Marita's hypnosis. Saagwalla was in a very grim mood. He was also full of questions. Why and where was Dr. Marita Von Svenson hiding? What had happened to Fern Verdant? His only comfort was in imagining the horrible torture he would inflict upon Marita once he found her.

Most people would have recognized this as a bad moment to have a chat with Saagwalla, but not Claude Hubris. Claude entered the cave and started blathering on about nothing at all. Even when Saagwalla was in the best of moods, he did not suffer fools gladly. He told Claude to shut up, but Claude did not. He kept rambling on out of sheer nervousness. Claude wondered aloud what Luella would prepare for dinner that evening. Last night, he told the doctor, they'd had the most astonishingly delicious squid.

"What," Henry Saagwalla growled, "did you say?"

Claude didn't understand why Saagwalla was so upset.

"We . . . um . . . had . . . um . . . some very delicious squid."

Sometimes the wrong word at the wrong time can set a person off. *Squid* was that wrong word! It pushed Saagwalla over the edge. When Henry Saagwalla thought of squid, he thought of *giant squid* and of Marita's ineptness and Fern's disappearance.

Henry Saagwalla turned to Hubris with a sickly fake smile and said how lucky Claude was to have such a wonderful wife looking after him. In fact, Saagwalla said, he was quite lonely in the evenings. Perhaps Luella might make them both dinner that night? Claude shut up immediately. He knew Luella would rather walk naked into a leech-infested swamp than have to spend an evening with Henry Saagwalla, but what could he say? He was too afraid of Saagwalla to say no. That night the Hubrises would join Saagwalla at his home, and Luella would cook.

Luella had a screaming fit when Claude broke the news. She was determined to make the worst dinner ever, so he'd never ask her to cook again. She prepared baked toad heads with sea urchin sauce, and raw egg-white soup with mouse ears. Claude and Luella were in the kitchen bickering when Henry Saagwalla dropped a sleeping potion into their martinis. When they returned to the table, Saagwalla proposed a toast to his gracious chefs. The Hubrises drank their cocktails, and within moments plummeted into unconsciousness.

Henry Saagwalla went to his laboratory door and punched in a long computer code. After a series of clicks, the door opened. Inside the laboratory were shelves filled with brightly colored liquids in all the shades of the rainbow. Some were phosphorescent and shone in the dark, others bubbled and gurgled, others fizzed and hissed. Mounted on the wall were rows of vials. There were hundreds of them. Each one was labeled. On the labels were things like *Sleep Forever, Wake Up Screaming, Toes Drop Off, Third Ear, Warble Instead of Speak,* on and on they went. Saagwalla plucked a vial of serum from the wall and left. The door locked behind him.

Back upstairs Claude and Luella were still flopped faces down at the dinner table. From a drawer, Henry Saagwalla drew a long needle. He filled it with serum from the vial and injected each of the Hubrises with half the serum. He rang for his albino sidekick, Leslie, to take the Hubrises back to the cave.

Albert Wedgie hated Claude and Luella for how they had treated him, so he was overjoyed when Leslie arrived in the cave, ferrying the unconscious Hubrises in a wheelbarrow. Although Albert was moving very slowly on his trunklike legs, he still managed to help Leslie construct a crude set of wooden bars in one corner of the cave. Saagwalla had ordered Leslie to hang a mirror in the tiny prison.

The next morning Luella awoke to find she was behind bars in the cave. Albert Wedgie stood smiling at her, or smiling as much as he could through a mouth that looked like a knot in a tree.

"What are you staring at, you idiot?" she barked.

With difficulty, Albert pointed toward the mirror. Luella turned and gazed at her reflection. She saw, to her horror, that not only was she completely without accessories, but her skin had taken on a light green pallor and her hair looked like weedy straw. She promptly screamed and fainted. Her scream awoke Claude Hubris, who took one look at Luella, and at the cave prison they were in, and screamed too.

"You can't do this! You'll never get away with this!"

"I can and I did and I will." Henry Saagwalla stepped from the shadows of the cave, smiling an oily smile. "You'd better get all of your talking done now, because your vocal abilities will be collapsing quite soon. I tripled the normal dosage, so the transformation will be a speedy one."

Claude Hubris's eyes grew wide. It was true. His jaw was already feeling slightly stiff. Leslie put tape over Claude's and Luella's mouths so Saagwalla didn't have to listen to them anymore.

"Thank goodness. Some peace and quiet! This mess wouldn't

have happened if you'd done your jobs properly. It's very difficult finding good help these days," he added.

Saagwalla turned his attention to Lily Verdant. The Silver Rose trembled on the table next to her. Lily sensed Saagwalla's presence, and it turned her blood cold.

"Well, things have taken an unexpected turn. Your daughter seems to be missing, but she must be on her way here, otherwise she wouldn't have been found bobbing around in the middle of the Pacific Ocean." Saagwalla took a deep breath. "No worries. All good things are worth waiting for."

Lily sent out a panicked message to Albert Wedgie.

"Tonight, Albert! It's time!" Albert agreed that he would do anything to help Lily escape.

Back in Singapore, Olivier and Serge Cransac landed at a private airfield owned and operated by the Singapore branch of the Resistance. After locating Marita's vessel with the aid of Resistance technology, they boarded the boat just as the two remaining henchthugs were preparing to push off. Marita had been sunbathing, using a foil reflecting sheet to absorb as much of the sun's rays as possible—either she had not heard of the dangers of excessive tanning, or she was making up for a lifetime of pallor. While Olivier barely recognized Marita Von Svenson, Marita recognized Olivier immediately, and she shouted at Oren to push off faster. She stood quickly, and her foil sheet fell to the ground. Then she stared at Olivier in a strange way. Olivier, now very aware of her reputation, turned away, shielding his eyes, but Serge was quickly falling under her spell. Olivier dropped to his knees and grabbed the reflective aluminum rectangle. He held it up directly in front of Marita; her big eyes shone right back at her. In a flash, Marita Von Svenson had hypnotized herself.

Without Marita ordering them around Oren and Igor didn't know what to do. The two henchthugs wandered aimlessly onto the dock and out into the bustle of Singapore. Olivier sat Marita down.

"You are hypnotized," he said, "and you will truthfully answer everything I ask you." Olivier decided to ask some simple questions to make sure she was thoroughly hypnotized.

"What's your name?"

"Dr. Marita Ingrid Elke Von Svenson."

"What is your profession?"

"I am a child psychiatrist whose methods are misunderstood by the world. I did my postgraduate specialization at the University of Abusive Psychoanalysis; my thesis was on the advanced mistreatment of children. I have escaped Nedlaw where I had the thankless job of keeping hundreds of insane children in line, of having to explain to mummy and daddy why little Britnee and Troy were hitting their heads against walls. While I love administering a good dose of electroshock therapy, even that was beginning to wear thin. Give, give, give, that's all I do. I'm about ready to move on and get a life. When I was offered this job . . . well, how could I refuse? I could retire, and have some fun for once."

Serge Cransac taped everything with his micro-recorder/computer. He waited a brief moment, then the verification flashed on the screen.

"It all checks out," he said. "Except that last bit . . . we have no way of knowing . . ."

Olivier was horrified. This was the woman he had entrusted with the care of his child.

"Where are Lily and Fern? Why have they been kidnapped?" asked Olivier.

"They were kidnapped because they talk to plants. They will help Henry Saagwalla control the world." Olivier was puzzled. His wife was a botanist and all botanists talked to plants. His daughter had simply been misunderstood. In any case, how on earth would either of them help anyone control the world? It was all absurd.

"Henry Saagwalla!" said Serge. "This is very bad."

"Where are they?" Olivier interrupted angrily.

"Lily Verdant . . . ," Marita said.

"Yes, yes . . . ?" said Olivier eagerly.

". . . is unconscious in a cave with Henry Saagwalla in Sri Lanka."

"She's alive!!!!" Olivier cried, overcome with relief. He could barely believe it was true, and had to stop himself from weeping with joy.

"And Fern . . . where is my daughter, Fern Verdant?"

Marita Von Svenson's glazed eyes focused on some dim point in the distance. The question registered with her.

"Fern Verdant is at the bottom of the ocean." Olivier's mouth fell open in disbelief. He slumped over as though someone had punched him in the stomach.

Nearly

Fern sat on the bow of the *Porpoise* as it moved toward the shoreline. The sea spray splashed in her face as the boat bounced in the waves. She and Tim had studied the maps; it was undeniable that the landmass they were heading toward was Sri Lanka. Fern searched for any piece of information on Sri Lanka that she could find.

She discovered that the island is full of jungles and rare vegetation. It is lush and beautiful, and therefore a very unusual place for a nature hater to use as a hideaway—or perhaps it was really the most clever place. As the *Porpoise* neared land Fern heard voices wafting out from the shore, floating over the waves toward her.

"Over here . . . over here," they whispered to her.

Glancing overboard, she saw the most extraordinarily

beautiful coral reef beneath the surface of the sea. It was brimming with bright swimming flashes of tropical fish; schools of silver, gold, blue, green, and red.

"Is she on that island?" Anthony came up behind her. Fern nodded, afraid to say anything in case she cried with happiness. Her mother was so near.

"Then I'm sure we'll find her," Anthony said. Then, "Those reefs are very delicate . . . it's better to moor away from them." Anthony dropped the anchor far enough away so it wouldn't harm the coral. Fern was impressed. For someone who had seemed so gruff, he was really very thoughtful.

Everyone piled into a small dinghy and headed toward the island. They landed on the most beautiful beach any of them had ever seen. Fern stepped into water that felt as warm as soup, just like in her long-ago dream in Paris. The sandy beach abutted a jungle so dense you could barely set foot in it. The fragrance of hibiscus, frangipani, and sandalwood escaped from the darkened canopy. Fern, Francesca, and Anthony set up camp. The sun was low on the horizon, setting behind them to the west. Fern and Francesca gathered dead branches and leaves for a fire, while Anthony explored the coast. The littlest orphans played in the surf, and Tim pored over his maps, discovering they had landed on the most remote part of the island.

Anthony walked up and down the shoreline as far as he could. "There's not a single hut or village anywhere," he reported.

"Maybe this whole island could be ours," Kai said. "It could be our new home." He didn't know that Sri Lanka already had a lot of people, just not here.

It was getting dark fast now. Anthony built a crackling fire on the beach. The orphans heated some cans of baked beans and ate them on fresh oatmeal bread that Lulu had baked onboard the boat that very morning. They gorged on pineapple and coconut as the flickering light from the fire played against their faces. Jane told a story about a boatload of orphans on a desert island who discovered a lost treasure. Everyone laughed as they recognized themselves in the story, except Fern, who was lost deep in thought . . . so deep that she jumped when a voice barged into her head.

"Fern?" The voice came from a little ways down the beach. "Fern Verdant?" the voice called out.

Fern followed the voice to the edge of the jungle. Anthony watched her out of the corner of his eye. A little way in from the beach, in the fading sunlight, she could see a pond. In the pond was a flower. It had a purple center, surrounded by a burst of yellow petals, which were ringed by more purple petals. It was beautiful.

Fern knelt down. "I'm Fern Verdant. Who are you?"

"Nymphaea Stellata," answered the purple beauty. "Stella's easier. I have news of your mother. Her message passed through us many months ago. The bloom that originally sent it is long gone, but we all know to watch out for you. We knew you would come."

"And she's . . . ?"

"Alive? Yes."

Fern breathed a sigh of relief. "Where is she?"

"In a cave," answered Stella, "beyond the jungle. But you

must be careful. It's extremely dangerous. You'll have no opposition from any vine or creeper, though; no one embraces the evil in that cave. The man in that cave is bent on destroying all plants of any kind."

Fern looked past the pond into the tangle of trees and vines. You could barely see a foot into it, it was so dense and dark.

"Thank you for this . . . and for sending the message. I am eternally grateful." Fern returned to the campfire and sat down beside Francesca.

"You must be so happy, knowing you'll see your mother soon," Francesca said.

"I can hardly believe it."

The moon shone down. Occasionally they heard the sound of a fish leaping out of the water and spiraling back in with a splash. They agreed that they would set out to find Fern's mother at dawn, while it was still cool. They needed sleep, and it was too dark to venture into the jungle at night. They would take turns guarding the camp.

Fern fell asleep with the others by the fire. Tim woke her up at about four in the morning so she could take over the guard post. As soon as Tim dozed off, Fern got up. She was very quiet as she wrote a note and placed it under a stone by the fire.

"Wait!" cried the Petal. "You can't leave me. We're a team. Now pick me up and bring me with you!"

Fern picked up her backpack.

"You're staying here. I don't want to put anyone else in danger."

"I'm going to have severe abandonment issues!"

"It's for the best," Fern said, and quickly set off, walking barefoot down to the beach, the Petal's protests fading behind her. She stepped into the surf to prevent leaving footprints and waded along in the water for nearly a mile. Dawn was approaching. She wanted some light before turning into the dark jungle.

When she woke up, Francesca discovered Fern's note, and woke the others. Anthony read it aloud.

" 'Dear friends, I cannot take you with me on the final leg of this journey, as I fear it will be very dangerous. I have already put you in harm's way too many times. So I ask you to wait for me, on the *Porpoise*. I will return with my mother as soon as I can. Please care for the Petal. Thank you for everything, and wish me well. Fern Verdant.' " The Petal sulked, but no one recognized the sulking of a metal petal.

Anthony traced Fern's footsteps down to the water's edge where they disappeared into the sea. There were no tracks anywhere. She could have gone in either direction.

"What should we do? She shouldn't go alone!" said Francesca. Anthony's gaze was fixed on the jungle; on the spot where he'd seen Fern disappear the night before.

When Fern crossed the beach toward the dense undergrowth, she was faced with a blockade of green. She'd never seen a jungle, let alone one so thick. Sounds flew from it: hoots, hollers, whooshes, croaks, hisses, yelps, and the crinkling of dead leaves and brush being stepped on by who knows what.

"What exactly is in that jungle?" Fern asked a nearby orchid.

"Elephants, monkeys, leopards, frogs, cobras, sloths, lizards as large as crocodiles, butterflies, and bats; lots and lots and lots of bats," the Orchid answered. "Oh. And bugs. Big bugs."

This was not good news. Fern tied her hair in one knot, and then another. She didn't want bats and bugs getting tangled in it. She pulled on her hiking boots and set one foot down in the pitch-black forest. That was it. She could go no farther, it was so dense. She tried to push back the vegetation, but it was impossible to move it even a foot. She could barely get her hand through the undergrowth, let alone her body. Fern contemplated asking the trees to pick her up as the Eucalyptus had done near Mystery, when she heard a noise like a deep, long groan. Fern nearly jumped out of her skin. The sound grew and grew, until it sounded as if the very earth were yawning open. Then, slowly, very slowly, the trees in front of her creaked and moaned, and began to part.

Vines, flowers, shrubs, and palms followed suit. Fern stepped back, unsure what exactly was happening. Gradually a pathway revealed itself through the center of the jungle.

"Hurry up!" the jungle plants urged her. "Hurry up!" Fern stepped gingerly onto the path, and into the thick growth. As she inched forward, the jungle corridor behind her closed up as tight as a vault. Looking back, she saw nothing but a wall of thick, black, impenetrable jungle. Even if they wanted to, no one would be able to follow her.

Fern followed the path. Eyes peered at her from the shadows. Parrots squawked from the treetops. She saw flashes of blue and red soar from branch to branch above her. The shifting foliage jumbled the sonar of one inexperienced bat, and it slammed into Fern's head, falling to the ground, dazed. From that vantage point it stared at Fern as if to say, "What are you doing in my jungle?" She could hear the whispering of the plants as she passed.

"Is that really Fern Verdant?"

"She's quite little, isn't she?"

"It's not about size. It's about the gift."

"Poor thing."

"Brave thing. It's so awfulllll!"

A little light made its way through the dense treetops and lit the path. The plant chatter continued innocuously, and Fern found it comforting. Animal sounds erupted here and there, but Fern continued onward, crunching down on dead palm fronds and leaves. The jungle was cool and damp. It smelled musty. Fern walked and walked, asking herself the same question over and over again: How would she possibly defeat Henry Saagwalla? She was so consumed by this question that she didn't notice when the jungle that had been filled with noises suddenly turned deathly quiet. The only sound was that of her own breathing, and then, something else, something that sounded almost like a distant dull saw.

Fern stopped in her tracks. The noise transformed into deep ragged breaths punctuated by a low growl. The growl grew louder.

"Look out above you!!!" a nearby Frangipani shouted. Fern turned her gaze upward and saw, twelve feet overhead, amid the tangle of vines, a leopard perched on a thick tree branch. It had incredible dark eyes, tan skin, and dark spots. It was beautiful. It was also at least nine feet long, its big teeth were bared in Fern's direction, and it was staring right at her. The leopard crouched lower on its haunches, watching her every move. Fern stood as still as a statue, remembering that she'd heard this was the thing to do when faced with a man-eating animal. She just couldn't remember which man-eating animal this worked for. Fern stared at the leopard. The leopard stared at Fern.

Fern realized she had forgotten to breathe. She let out a little breath, and then . . . she blinked. The leopard detected this tiniest of movements. It rose on its haunches, its jaws unhinging slightly, its teeth glistening. It sprung from the limb, arching up in the air—beautiful, except for its huge fangs. Its front paws were extended toward Fern's face. Leopard saliva dropped onto Fern's cheek. Fern fell to her knees; she crossed her arms over her head, closing her eyes. How stupid it was to have made it this far only to find herself leopard lunch. Then she heard a piercing yowl. She opened her eyes, and looked up. The leopard dangled in the air a few inches above her. Its paws swiped out at her. Fern ducked, and the paws sliced through the air, missing her by an inch. A thick vine had wrapped itself around the leopard's tail and held on as tightly as it could. The leopard bobbed above her like a yo-yo, occasionally curling back on itself to take a swipe at the Vine. The Vine wriggled and writhed like a live bungee cord, and Fern could have sworn she heard laughter, as if the Vine was having great fun. Fern crawled on her hands and knees, leaving the bobbing beast far behind her. Then she stumbled to her feet and ran panting through the jungle until she could no longer hear its yowls.

Meanwhile . . . Again

After the orphans found Fern's note, there was some discussion as to what their next move would be.

Tim pored over his maps, trying to determine where Fern might have gone in light of the fact the jungle was so dense you could barely poke a stick in it.

Kai was annoyed at being left behind. "She drags us halfway around the world and then disappears! Just when the best part of the adventure is starting!"

"She was only trying to protect us," said Francesca.

"I think she's terribly brave," said Jane. "It must be wonderful to have your own personal quest."

Lulu was worried about Fern alone in the jungle and tried to distract herself by inventing a recipe for coconut pancakes. Anthony was quiet for a minute.

"You'll return to the *Porpoise* and wait for her."

"What do you mean, 'you'?" asked Francesca.

"Once I make sure you're all safely on board the boat, I'm going to see if she needs help," he announced. "After all, she came back for us, and Francesca wouldn't be here without her help."

Francesca looked at her brother. The expression on his face told her there was no use arguing with him. They all climbed into the dinghy, and set out. Halfway to the boat the dinghy nearly capsized because of the ridiculous number of coconuts Lulu had squirreled away on board. After dumping twenty-seven coconuts into the Indian Ocean, they arrived back at the *Porpoise*. Anthony prepared to return to shore.

Back in Singapore, Olivier Verdant was devastated. He couldn't believe that his daughter lay at the bottom of the ocean, even though a cold, heartless, and hypnotized Marita Von Svenson had said this was the case. Marita's powers of hypnosis were so potent that she remained firmly under her own spell. Nevertheless, Olivier didn't want to risk the possibility of her snapping out of it and hypnotizing everyone in sight. He put dark sunglasses on her, and blinders—the type you would put on race-horses so their neighbors on the track don't distract them. As tempted as Olivier was to toss Marita Von Svenson into the Straits of Singapore, he knew he would need her in the future. So Olivier and Serge Cransac took Marita to the Resistance's secret landing strip and bundled her into the back of their airplane, then took off for Sri Lanka to find Lily. Olivier dreaded the moment he would have to tell his wife of the horrible end of her only child.

"Who are the Hubrises?" Olivier asked Marita as they left Singapore.

"The Hubrises are two rose-growing idiots who were hired by Henry Saagwalla to develop a spectacular rose in order to lure Lily Verdant."

"And who exactly is Henry Saagwalla?"

"Henry Saagwalla is a brilliant man who will one day control the entire world." As their plane flew over the Indian Ocean, Dr. Marita Von Svenson would not shut up.

"He was the teacher's assistant in one of my undergrad classes at Oxford. He was brilliant. We all worshipped him, but I was his favorite student . . . ," Marita sighed. "Now, of course, he'll kill me if he gets ahold of me. I'll tell you a secret, only because I can't stop myself. I always had a little crush on him. He wasn't much to look at, but what a mind!"

Olivier had had enough. "Be quiet!" he ordered her. Marita followed his command; her mouth shut like a clam.

Olivier gazed out of the low-flying plane. As glum as he was, he couldn't help but notice the color of the water, which was the most beautiful he had ever seen. Even from this vantage point he could see massive beds of seaweed. It almost looked as though they were waving at him. The botanist in him couldn't help but be interested. There's a saying among botanists: once a botanist, always a botanist, even if you become an international secret agent. As Olivier gazed out the passenger window of the plane, he saw an orange boat floating below. He pulled out his super-powered Resistance binoculars and looked down.

"How odd! There's an orange boat with a deck full of children floating below us." He read aloud the name on the side of the bow. "The *Porpoise?*"

Dr. Marita Von Svenson squealed through sealed lips.

"What?" Olivier looked over at her. But she was still under the command to be silent. "Okay," Olivier sighed. "Speak!"

"The *Porpoise!*" The words burst from Dr. Marita Von Svenson's lips like a river overflowing its banks. "Impossible. I set the *Porpoise* on fire. It was manned by a group of belligerent and useless orphans. One of these useless orphans, Francesca somebody-or-other, escaped from NITPIC at the same time as Fern. I found your daughter on the *Porpoise* with the orphans and I snatched her, but she stupidly hurled herself overboard from the *Barracuda* and drowned . . . proving just how mentally unstable she really was. Whatever you're looking at can't be the *Porpoise*, because it was burned to a crisp." Olivier peered through the binoculars again.

"It may be toasted, but it's definitely the *Porpoise*, and if I am counting correctly there are six children on its deck." It suddenly occurred to Olivier that if Marita Von Svenson was wrong about the *Porpoise*, she might possibly be wrong about Fern. Olivier took another look through the binoculars.

"Those children all need electro-sock therapy. My most recent invention," added Dr. Marita Von Svenson. "At NITPIC I had all the socks of the disobedient wired so I could give them a good blast of shock by remote control. I think I might patent that and sell it. There must be millions of irritated parents around the world who'd love to use it on their bad children."

"Be quiet!" Olivier commanded. Marita immediately shut up.

Below them, on the deck of the *Porpoise*, the six orphans looked up at the plane.

"Ahoy, there!" Olivier called out through a megaphone, as the airplane buzzed over them. "Do any of you know the whereabouts of Fern Verdant?" Olivier continued. "This is her father, Olivier Verdant."

Down below Kai frowned. "I told you a non-orphan would get us in trouble." Then the voice boomed out of the plane again as it circled once more.

"We've been told she's dead. Please wave if . . . if there is any possibility my daughter is still alive?"

Anthony had one foot in his dinghy and was preparing to return to shore to look for Fern when he heard the announcement. He looked around at his crew, taking a silent consensus.

"We can't very well let her father believe she's dead when she's not," said Francesca. "Can we?"

No one moved for the longest time. They looked at one another, afraid of the far-reaching consequences making contact might have. The plane flew in anxious circles above them. No one wanted to be sent back to an orphanage, or end up homeless on the streets. But everyone knew they had to do the right thing—except Kai. Very hesitantly, Anthony raised his hand and waved up to Olivier.

In the plane, Olivier turned to Serge. There were tears in his eyes.

"She's alive, Serge!" he said. "Fern's alive."

Serge gave him the thumbs-up and took the plane in a joyful loop-de-loop.

The Cave

Fern emerged from the jungle coughing and sputtering and realizing she'd need more exercise in the future, especially if she was to travel the world in aid of plants. She fell to her knees to catch her breath. Ahead of her lay a beautiful sight. In the distance, to the right, lush green hills rose. To the left were strange plateaus, carved from rose quartz that sparkled in the sunlight like mountains of pink diamonds. Fern had never seen anything like it. A rough path wound through the center of the hills and the plateaus. Past the green and the pink, the path led to pure darkness. Voices floated to her from a nearby group of orchids.

"Thissss wayyyy," the Orchids chanted. "The cave is thissss way." Fern started down the path, the green hills on one side and the pink quartz on the other. As she walked, she noticed a most peculiar thing. Nestled in the hills were trees pruned in the shape of a boy with a gentle smile on his face, sitting cross-legged. Opposite, in the pink plateaus, she saw the same beautiful boy carved into the rose quartz. From both sides the smiling boy looked down on her as she walked along the dusty path. His presence made her feel safe.

Tiny blue monkeys with white faces and worried eyes darted out of the hills onto the path around her. Holding hands, they danced in frantic little circles, chittering and chattering. Ahead of her, the path snaked back and forth. She was just thinking how beautiful and pleasant this all was when she rounded a bend and everything changed. The monkeys were gone, vanishing as quickly as they'd appeared. Green hills and pink quartz dissolved into a blackened landscape. Dark clouds hovered above. A jagged, rocky escarpment loomed ahead. Several gaping caves yawned at its base. The flowers and grasses lining the path shook convulsively, pointing to one opening in particular. Above, the sky looked like spilled ink, even though it was midday.

Fern approached the cave cautiously. A cold breeze blew out of the gloom. There were only a few weary plants at its mouth, all others too fearful to root. The stalwarts bowed as she approached.

"Is my mother, Lily Verdant, in there?" she whispered to a straggly length of grass.

"Yessss," said the Grass.

"Thank goodness," Fern sighed with relief.

"Goodness has nothing to do with it," the Grass said.

"What do you mean?"

"Evil," the Grass said, bending in the direction of the gloomy cave.

A chill poured from the darkness. Fern took the Vapor-icer out of her backpack; she would freeze Saagwalla, render him harmless forever, and rescue her mother. When she looked at the Vapor-icer in her hand, she saw she was shaking like a leaf.

A thought burst into her consciousness. "Shaking like a leaf!" Off in the distance a tree had heard her thoughts. "Are you insinuating trees are afraid?"

"No! No! Sorry," said Fern. "It's an old expression"—she paused—"that I will never be using again."

"Better not," the Tree said.

Fern took a breath and inched her way into the entrance. It was very dark, but she didn't want to use a flashlight and announce her arrival. She paused in the entryway, waiting for her eyes to adjust to the dimness. The place smelled damp and musty. Shapes began to appear in the gloom. Salamanders slithered across the cool rock. Big black spiders dangled from the ceiling, performing acrobatic feats. Water dripped monotonously somewhere in the distance. Fern could see why someone with an evil plot would choose this place as their headquarters. No one in their right mind would want to venture down here. Fern proceeded slowly, her hands slipping off the slimy walls as she felt her way forward. Her eyes adjusted to the darkness and she could just make out the width and height of the passageway. It was wide enough to drive a car through, and towered above her, disappearing into darkness.

Fern inched her way into the cave, placing one foot carefully in front of the other. The pounding of her heart boomed in her ears, intensifying every time she had to brush a creepy-crawly thing out of her path. Her imagination ran wild. She pictured spiders the size of bicycles emerging from the recesses of the cave.

"There is nothing to be afraid of. There is nothing to be afraid of," she repeated to herself over and over. Soon, the only thing Fern heard was her own voice. "There is nothing to be afraid of. There is nothing to be afraid of." Everything else had gone very quiet, except . . . except for someone's breathing . . . someone other than Fern. She looked over her shoulder, and all around her. No one. Shrinking back against the wall, she surveyed the length of the corridor. There was nothing there. Above her, the ceiling was too dark and high to see anything but pure blackness. The sound persisted, as though the very walls of the cave were inhaling and exhaling. The goose bumps on her arms grew bigger. The sound breathed down her neck.

Fern started walking faster now, tripping and sliding on rocks, desperate to get away from the breath that filled every inch of the cave. She rounded another bend, and the cave became slightly brighter, making it a little easier to identify the shapes in the murkiness. Fern turned her gaze to the roof of the cave. She stopped in her tracks, frozen. There, suspended above her, were bats. Not a couple. Not a few hundred. There were at least a thousand bats hanging from the roof, their little bat wings enveloping them like tiny upside-down mummies. Every bat head was tilted in Fern's direction.

Two thousand bat eyes watched Fern watch them. She flung her arms over her head to protect herself. But they didn't move one inch. While she waited for them to come screaming from the ceiling in her direction, a much bigger sound came lumbering through the cave. It was a scraping, dragging, heaving sound. Fern tore her attention away from the bats and onto the light down the passageway. Heading toward her, lurching on massive, unsteady legs, was a hideous monster.

The creature had a man shape, but its legs were like thick trunks, and roots trailed from them. Its arms were like branches, and leaves sprouted from its head. It was moving very slowly; each step seemed more laborious than the last. Fern put her finger on the trigger of the Vapor-icer. The figure dragged itself closer and closer. The weapon shook in Fern's hand. As the figure staggered nearer, Fern saw the very frightened eyes of what appeared to be a man trapped in a tree's body. She pointed the Vapor-icer at the creature's head. It looked at her, petrified, and then, with a hint of recognition, it spoke to her telepathically. "You're the daughter of Lily Verdant!"

Fern's mouth fell open in surprise. "Yes . . . I'm Fern Verdant."

"You look just like your mother." The poor creature looked like it was going to collapse, and that's exactly what it did, creaking like a small tree falling over.

"What are you?" Fern asked. "I mean, who are you?"

"Please . . . please, you must read this letter." The creature flopped a branchlike arm in Fern's direction. "This will explain everything. It took me ages to write. Your mother dictated it."

Fern took a white envelope from the tree-man's grip. She could hear the creature's labored breathing. The letter was written in a scratchy, jagged style.

Dear Whoever,

I am a missing botanist being held captive in a cave. I am convinced I will be the subject of a terrible experiment, just as this poor messenger, Albert Wedgie, has been. I wish only to be reunited with my daughter, Fern, and my beloved husband, Olivier Verdant. Please contact the authorities and have Albert Wedgie direct you to the cave where I am hidden. He has been a good and loyal friend and we must help him too. Henry Saagwalla, a master of evil, is my torturer. Beware of him. Protect yourself.

I am at your mercy.

Lily Verdant

Fern reread it. She couldn't believe her mother was so near. Folding the letter up, she returned it to the envelope.

"You poor creature." She knelt down beside Albert Wedgie, patting his rough, barky forehead. "What did they do to you?"

"Henry Saagwalla gave me one of his serums. I've turned into a horrible freak. I'm a . . . a . . . Plan . . . or a Mant . . . I don't know which."

"I'm so sorry."

"Your mother said she'd help me get back to who I was."

"My mother is good at helping plants, and I'm sure she'll be able to help you. Now, if I can get you up on your feet, do you think you can keep going?"

Albert Wedgie slowly nodded his barky head.

"Then you must take this letter out of the cave and try to find some help." She handed the envelope back to Albert, placing it in one of his leafy limbs.

"I'll try my best."

Fern took some of her water and poured it into Albert's dry, barky mouth.

"I trimmed my roots before the trip, but they're growing again. I have no idea how much time I have left . . . ," Albert trailed off, not wanting to imagine his fate. Fern heaved and tugged, pulling him up so he was leaning against the wall of the cave. He was quite heavy.

Fern watched as Albert struggled to put one tree leg in front of the other. "You are very brave," she called as he lumbered slowly away.

Fern continued her journey down the cave, toward the light. She looked up at the bats, their eyes boring into her quietly. They still hadn't budged an inch. They just watched and waited, for what, she didn't know. Fern clung to the shadows of the cave walls. The cave was becoming lighter and lighter. Outside she heard a low rumbling noise. At first, dulled by the thick rock wall of the cave, it sounded like thunder. Then she recognized it as some kind of plane engine. She hesitated. Should she go back to the mouth of the cave and try to signal for help, or proceed on to her mother? Ahead of Fern the tunnel opened wider.

"Down here! Please, help us! Down here!" A voice grated from the opening. There was something familiar in the tone of the voice. It was metallic, just like the Silver Petal. "I am the Silver Rose! Please help us!" Fern was beside herself. She was so close. There was no way she was turning back now. Fern hurried down the passageway. The ceiling of bats receded behind her. She heard the low mumbling of voices filtering through the gloom. The tunnel widened and she found herself at the mouth of an inner cave. She crouched down, hidden in the shadows, and spied.

The opening led to a huge cavern. On the far side of the cavern, Fern saw a dark-haired man in a white lab coat, bent low. There was a body in front of him, lying on a gurney, but Fern couldn't see it properly because his back was blocking her view. She shifted to the right, lying flat on her belly. Then she saw something awful. Long black curls, like Lily's curls but with a streak of silver, spilled over the side of the gurney. Fern bit her tongue to stop herself from screaming. Lily's wrists and ankles were strapped down. Across from the dark-haired man was a short albino. In his hand was a surgical knife.

"Ready when you are, Mr. Saagwalla," said Leslie.

"Hmmm . . . I could remove the brain, store it, and have the knowledge extracted," answered Saagwalla. "I know of a laboratory in Vladivostok that's experimented with such things."

Fern gasped, but so did someone else. Saagwalla turned around, looking toward the corner of the cave. Fern followed his gaze and saw a makeshift prison built into the rock. It contained the quickly foliating Hubrises. They stared wide-eyed and leafy at Fern Verdant. Fern didn't recognize the Hubrises, but they recognized her. Fern shrank back into the shadows. Claude and Luella would have screamed, except that Saagwalla had instructed Leslie to duct-tape their mouths. He had grown tired of Luella shrieking and of Claude saying over and over again, "You'll never get away with this," when Saagwalla knew perfectly well he would. All the Hubrises could do now was make noises. Henry Saagwalla turned to his talkative prisoners.

"Shut up!" He refocused on Lily. "I'm wondering if we should remove the whole head, and not just the brain," Saagwalla spoke across the table to Leslie. "It could come in handy later on."

"You know best," Leslie nodded.

Fern couldn't believe what she'd just heard. *Remove the brain! Remove the head!* She couldn't take it anymore. She sprang to her feet.

"Get away from my mother!" Fern ran out from the shadows. She aimed the Vapor-icer at Saagwalla's back. Her hand was trembling. Then, she noticed something peculiar. Saagwalla's shoulders were shaking . . . with laughter. He put down his surgical equipment and turned to face her, trying to stifle a laugh.

"I said, move away from her!" Fern called out, confused by this odd reaction. "You are not removing her brain!"

225

"Of course I'm not." A smug smile spread across his face.

"But . . . but . . . ," stammered Fern.

"We were putting on a little show for you. Did you really think we'd saw into her brain? With that remarkable gift, I don't think so. Now say hi to mommy." Saagwalla stepped away from the sleeping Lily. Fern's comatose mother lay inert, the Silver Rose glinting beside her on a table.

Fern pointed the Vapor-icer at Saagwalla.

"Get away from that gurney!"

"Certainly," said Saagwalla, looking at Fern. Fern could now see that his face was disfigured, but that wasn't what frightened her. What frightened her was the look in his eyes.

"You, too," she ordered Leslie the albino assistant.

"Don't trust them," rasped the Silver Rose.

"I don't," responded Fern telepathically, adding, "Nice to finally meet you."

"Likewise," said the Rose.

"Is my mother all right?"

The Silver Rose found itself in the unusual position of being a translator between mother and daughter, since both Verdants could speak telepathically with plants, but not with other humans.

"I'm fine for a woman in a coma," Lily said through the Rose. "But what on earth are you doing here, young lady?" Fern had no time to respond.

"We'd thought we'd lost you," interrupted Saagwalla, "but the bats were kind enough to give us a heads-up. I've been

226

tracking your mother for quite some time. You are the bonus prize. I'm so fascinated by the entire phenomenon. How many generations of your family have had your 'talent'? It must be genetic. Perhaps your mother was exposed to some strange, extraterrestrial dust? So many questions to answer!" Saagwalla took a step toward Fern.

"I don't know what you're talking about, Henry Saagwalla," replied Fern. The scientist's expression turned dark and more evil than usual. "That's Mr. Saagwalla to you. I demand respect. I am a genius . . . and you . . . are only a freak of nature." Saagwalla took another step toward her.

The idea of freezing a person to death was horrifying, but Fern didn't see any other option. She had to get her mother out of here. Stepping toward Saagwalla, Fern tried to gauge exactly how far away she was from him. As she was very well aware, the Vapor-icer had a five-foot limit. Raising the gun, she pointed it at Saagwalla.

Saagwalla put his lips together as if he was whistling, but no sound came out. It unnerved Fern.

"What are you doing?" Fern asked.

Saagwalla ignored her and continued to purse his soundless lips. Fern knew that whatever he was up to, it was not good. Saagwalla took another step in Fern's direction.

"I warned you!" Fern squeezed the trigger and shot the Vapor-icer directly at Saagwalla. The jet of vapor flowed toward him, but he didn't move. He stood completely unfazed, smiling a creepy smile. A sound like a whoosh of air escaped from somewhere in the cave behind Fern. In less than a second, a swarm of bats had appeared, swooping down in front of Fern and creating a barrier protecting Saagwalla from the vapor. But they needn't have bothered. Fern had misjudged the distance. The ice flowed toward Saagwalla. Then suddenly it stopped, a quarter of an inch in front of the bats, forming a wall. The wall began to melt rapidly, creating a puddle at Fern's feet. The bats looked very relieved at this fortunate turn of events.

"I'd say you had equipment failure," Saagwalla said. With that, Leslie, in an awesome display of martial arts technique, spun across the room like an albino pinwheel, hands and feet flying. He seized the Vapor-icer from her hand. Leslie now held the weapon firmly in his grip. Fern stood helpless. Bats flew at her from every direction. Spiny black wings whipped around her head. She swatted at them, knocking their shiny bodies away, but there were too many for Fern's blows to have any effect. Bats tangled in her hair. She tugged at them, trying to pull them out. She could barely see. She opened her mouth and let out an earth-shattering scream.

The scream reverberated off the rock walls. The Hubrises cringed at the pitch. The Silver Rose quaked in its pot. Somewhere down the tunnel, Albert Wedgie heard it, and on the gurney, just a few feet away from Fern, Lily Verdant's eyes snapped open. She blinked several times.

"Fern?" Lily croaked, in the dry, hoarse voice of someone who had not spoken in months.

Everything else in the room fell silent. The bats, Saagwalla, Leslie, Fern—not a peep came from any of them.

"Mom?" The circling bats forming a whirling bat funnel around Fern halted mid-whirl.

Saagwalla couldn't believe his ears. He stared at the newly awakened Lily and at the captive Fern, and smiled.

"Well, good things certainly do come to those who wait!"

Reunited

Saagwalla ordered the bats away from Fern. The curtain of inky wings spiraled away from their prisoner. Fern rushed to her mother's side.

"Won't they escape?" Leslie whispered.

"The mother can barely sit up, let alone escape, you twit!" Saagwalla was quite thrilled. With both mother and daughter in his grasp, his access to the mysteries of their gift was certain. However, since he didn't exactly know what form their connection to plants took, he couldn't possibly know that Fern and Lily were already engaged in a telepathic conversation using the Silver Rose as a conduit.

"Mom!" cried Fern, through the Rose. Fern was frightened by Lily's pale and feeble condition. "Are you all right?" Lily was indeed very weak. Fern unshackled Lily's wrists and ankles. She helped her mother to sit up. The two of them hugged each other tightly, still not uttering a word aloud.

"I'm fine . . . but you shouldn't have come here, it's too dangerous," said Lily. "I sent specific instructions!"

"Would you have ignored a call from a threatened species?" Fern asked her mother. Lily could see Fern's point. "Besides, you don't look well. Why don't you get angry with me when you're feeling stronger?"

"Well, it's true, I have been in a coma, and that can be taxing," Lily replied. She glanced over to the Silver Rose.

"I wouldn't have survived if it hadn't been for the companionship of this wonderful flower." Since the Silver Rose was communicating this message to Fern, it blushed at the compliment, though *blush* may be the wrong word—it actually turned a beautiful metallic lavender color.

"If it weren't for your mother, I would have perished in the house of Hubris," said the Silver Rose.

"I know where your missing Silver Petal is. It's safe," Fern told the Rose.

The Rose sighed with relief. Saagwalla stared at the silently hugging mother and daughter.

"Mom, will it always feel strange to talk like this?"

"No. It's very odd at first, but you'll get used to it."

"All sweetness and light, isn't it?" Saagwalla said, irritated.

"How come they're not saying anything?" asked Leslie suspiciously.

Saagwalla was as puzzled by this as Leslie, but he wasn't about to acknowledge it, so he cuffed his associate on the ear.

"You must have so many questions, so many things you want to ask me! I feel terrible that I wasn't there for you when . . . ," Lily faltered.

"Please, Mom, don't worry. I'm figuring it out as I go along. The Trumpet Flower you left behind was very helpful." Fern looked around the cave. "How are we going to get out of here?"

"There's a poor creature with a plea for help who left here not long ago." Lily could barely sit up, let alone plot an escape.

"Albert Wedgie. I passed him. He's a brave man . . . er, tree." Fern took her mother's hand.

Everything was silent in the cave, except for the sound of vibrating bat wings in the distance and the occasional mumblings of the Hubrises. Saagwalla's eyes bored into the two mute Verdants. It dawned on Fern that this must look peculiar to the bystanders.

"How could you do this to her?" She turned on Saagwalla angrily. "Look at her! She's too peaked and weak to utter a single word!"

"Those two incompetents did this to her." Saagwalla pointed over at the makeshift prison that held what was left of the two Hubrises. Luella's hair looked like wild weeds, her face was barky, and her eyes and nose were knotty. She tried to point a creaky finger at Saagwalla, but the wood was too brittle, and her finger fell off. Claude Hubris had skin like polished ebony. Leaves grew from his head in a giant green pompadour. Neither of them could speak—they just made grunting, gasping sounds.

Fern realized they were turning into plants, just like Albert Wedgie.

232

"Their ineptitude will end here," added Saagwalla.

"Are those the horrible Hubrises?" Fern asked the Silver Rose.

"What's left of them," said the Rose.

"Oh my goodness!!!!!" A squawk came from across the room. It was Luella Hubris. She couldn't speak, but the words registered clearly in Fern's and Lily's minds.

"Good grief, Claude, she's talking about us . . . to a plant!"

"Incredible!" came Claude's voice.

"Unbelievable!" exclaimed Luella.

"Remarkable!" added Claude.

"That's their gift!" Claude and Luella shrieked in unison. "They can talk to plants telepathically!"

Luella fell silent. The realization hit her. "But, we can understand them, Claude. *We* can understand them too."

Claude turned to his wife. "Because we're becoming plants? Aghhhhh!!!!"

Sap streamed from Luella's knotty eyes. Their telepathic shrieks gave Lily and Fern massive headaches. A final burst of frenetic grunts and groans spat out of the Hubrises as their ability to talk as humans ebbed.

"They're a little noisy right now, but it'll stop soon. No sunlight equals no photosynthesis equals no plants . . . equals no Hubrises. Peace at last. No loose ends." Saagwalla sighed. "And . . . speaking of loose ends, what have you done with Marita Von Svenson?"

"I didn't do anything," Fern said. "She probably ran away so she wouldn't be turned into a radish."

Fern couldn't help staring at the Hubrises. Although she disliked them, she still thought that theirs was a terrible fate. Saagwalla was right, there was no natural light. Nothing could grow in this cave. Not a single plant, shrub, vine, or patch of greenery anywhere. What a nasty, slow death!

"She'll wish she was a radish by the time I get through with her," said Saagwalla. "Now, it's time to get down to business— time for the two of you to do a little talking."

"My mother's been in a coma for months. The least you can do is give her something nourishing and get her to a warmer, brighter place. This cave is a tomb." Fern was furious. "You're a monster, and you're killing her, and if she dies, so does her secret!"

"So, you do have a 'secret'?" Saagwalla smiled.

"Everyone has secrets," Fern said mysteriously.

"And your mother will tell me hers if she wants you to live! Most mothers will do anything to protect their children." He angrily thought back to the neglect he'd suffered at his own mother's hands, and realized there were exceptions. Saagwalla nodded in Leslie's direction. Leslie performed another series of blurry cartwheels punctuated by a couple of rapid-fire kicks into the air and landed behind Fern. He tied her hands with a cord, lifted her up with one hand, and dropped her in a chair near Saagwalla. He put Lily across from her in another chair.

"Now, Lily Verdant, tell me *how* it is you know when there's a croaking crocus in Canada, or a dying dahlia in Denmark?" Saagwalla nodded to Leslie, who now wielded a giant hypodermic needle. He stepped over to Fern. "Or do you want your daughter to grow feathers and squawk? It's hard enough being a teenager these days, without the additional liability of being a pigeon-girl."

"I'm not going to let them hurt you. I'll tell them the secret and they'll let you go," Lily said.

"You can't do that!" cried Fern. All Saagwalla heard was silence.

"Stop with this deafening silence!" Irritated, he nodded to Leslie, who set the needle against Fern's flesh. Everyone stared at everyone else.

"I'll tell you, I'll tell you," Lily blurted out loud.

"No, Mom!"

"I won't let them harm you." Lily looked at her daughter. There was no question in Lily Verdant's mind. She would tell the truth and lose the gift, before any harm could come to her daughter.

"It is my secret and my secret alone," Lily lied. "It has nothing to do with Fern." Lily sighed. "I can—" A faint sound permeated the walls of the cave, interrupting Lily. Henry Saagwalla looked up, and listened. He heard the unmistakable drone of an airplane engine buzzing low over the plateau.

"You can *what?*" Saagwalla asked impatiently. "You can what?"

The plane droned louder. Perhaps Albert Wedgie had delivered his message to someone, anyone. The pilot was obviously circling low, looking for something. The plane was very close by.

"Help!!!! Help!!!!" Fern shrieked at the thick rock walls.

Saagwalla gave her a look that could kill. The plane was now directly overhead. The piercing sound of an alarm rang through the cave. Leslie spun across the rocky length to a flashing yellow light on the wall. He turned off the alarm, smashed a glass case, and retrieved another, larger Vapor-icer. Saagwalla nodded at Leslie.

"Escape Plan A," Saagwalla ordered.

Leslie took aim and fired at everything in the cave. He blasted at the gurney, tables, chairs, and cabinets. Everything that was not a natural part of the cave was turned to ice. A crust of ice two feet thick formed on the walls and the ceiling.

Saagwalla removed a small control panel from his pocket. On it twenty buttons flashed in different colors. He pressed the largest button. There was an enormous grinding sound as a panel of rock slid open in the ground ahead of them. It revealed steps that led beneath the earth to a track. The track disappeared down a long, well-lit tunnel. On the track was a small train. Attached to the engine was a row of open carts, the type used in underground mines. Leslie scooped the fragile Lily off her chair and carried her down to the train, then lowered her into one of the carts.

Fern looked around the cave. It was more like the Arctic than Sri Lanka. Everything was white and frosty. Fern's teeth were chattering. But the ice didn't stay ice very long. In fact, it started melting moments after freezing, leaving no trace of its former shape. Iced chairs dripped into pools. Everything was melting into giant puddles of water. Drip, drip, dripping echoed through the cave and down the tunnel. There was only one little corner of unadulterated rock: the prison that held the Hubrises.

"What should I do about them?" Leslie nodded in the Hubrises' direction. Fern struggled in her chair.

"Get rid of them," answered Saagwalla. "They're loose ends."

Fern watched, horrified, as Leslie aimed the Vapor-icer and pulled the trigger. Almost instantly the Hubrises took on the appearance of oddly human trees crystallized by snow on a winter's day. Leslie grabbed Fern. She kicked as he carried her down the stairs in his meaty arms and deposited her in a cart. The Silver Rose was placed beside her.

Leslie returned to the cave. Both he and Saagwalla were riveted by the spectacle of the melting Hubrises. A tear formed in Saagwalla's eye. "Science is such a wonderful thing." Leslie nodded in agreement.

Meanwhile, down in the tunnel, Fern turned to the Silver Rose.

"Hold out your thorns!" The Rose did as ordered. It craned toward Fern, who extended her bound hands. Fern moved the cords binding her wrists across the metallic thorns. The thorns were like the teeth of a saw, and it took only a moment for them to saw through the rope. Fern crawled to the small engine of the train. A green button flashed "GO." Fern pressed down on it as hard as she could, and the train flew forward.

"Be careful," Lily warned from behind her. "You're too young to drive."

Above them, in the cave, puddles were rapidly forming on

the ground. Saagwalla and Leslie watched as more bits of the Hubrises melted. Soon the cave would be full of nothing but puddles. There was a bumping sound as the circling plane landed on the escarpment above them. The landing masked the sound of the train engine below. The airplane engine stopped, jolting Saagwalla and Leslie out of their reverie.

"Hurry up!" Saagwalla said. "Let's get out of here."

Saagwalla stepped through the opening in the floor, only to find that his train was disappearing down the tunnel. Water seeped from above and puddles were beginning to form on the track. Saagwalla pursed his lips, blowing his silent whistle. Almost instantly a whoosh of wings flew from the dark recesses of the cave. The bats poured down into the subterranean opening after Saagwalla and Leslie. The rock floor above them closed, leaving nothing at all but a cave filled with puddles, and the two melting Hubrises.

Fern's hand was on the throttle. While she didn't know how to drive, she could certainly read. The controls read *Fast, Faster, Fastest,* and *Stop,* so it was pretty easy to figure out. She moved the throttle to *Fastest.* A sound like a whipping wind followed them through the tunnel. Except it wasn't wind. It was the sound of thousands of bats flying underground. Lily ducked as they zoomed overhead like tiny rat jets, dive-bombing and swooping. Cuts and bat bites covered Fern's arms. Lily swatted the bats away as best she could. The train moved so fast that Fern's hair was whipped into a frenzy. The Silver Rose could barely think. It was in a state of shock from the excessive speed.

"Whhhhere do you think this track goes?" it asked.

"Away from Saagwalla," Fern answered. The train sped on for miles. Tunnels branched out into different areas, leading in all directions. It was a very complex underground system; Lily was quite impressed. The tracks, however, only lined the main tunnel. For ten minutes the train sped like a bullet, finally leaving the bats behind. Fern kept a careful lookout ahead. The train had headlights, but the tunnel itself was dark and creepy, and it was impossible to know what was around the next bend. Then the train rounded a curve, and Fern saw that the only thing lying ahead of them was a sheer rock wall!

The train sped toward the wall. Lily and Fern both screamed.

Fern jammed the throttle to *Stop*. The train skidded, sparks flying where the locked wheels screeched along the tracks. The Silver Rose flew out of the cart, and it crashed into a tunnel wall. The screeching sound filled the entire tunnel. Fern refused to believe that this would be the end of them. She closed her eyes and pulled at the throttle with all her strength. Her mother's hand squeezed her shoulder for support. Then abruptly, the train jolted to a stop. The two Verdants were vaulted out of the carts and onto the ground. When Fern opened her eyes, she discovered the train was two inches from the rock wall. She'd forgotten to breathe, and now she gasped for air. Lily opened her eyes and hugged her daughter in relief.

The Silver Rose lay behind them on the ground. It had oxidized into a ghastly green from fright.

"Are you all right?" Fern asked the Rose. But there was only silence in response.

"The poor thing's unconscious—probably traumatized. I know I am." Lily picked up the Silver Rose. "We'll just have to talk like everyone else."

On the wall beside them Fern saw a button. There was nothing else, anywhere, but rock—and a button. Fern and Lily exchanged a glance.

"I feel like Alice in Wonderland." With that, Fern pressed the button. A door in the rock slid open beside them. Narrow stairs led upward. There was really nowhere else for Fern and Lily and the Silver Rose to go. Lily leaned against the wall for support, hugging the Rose close. They made their way up the steep and winding stairs, at the top of which was another button. Fern pushed it. A door swung open. They entered a huge circular foyer that was paneled in dark ebony wood. Doors led to different wings of the building. Nearby, a window was open. Lily inhaled. It was the first fresh air she had breathed in months.

"We're near the sea," she sighed. Mother and daughter looked at each other. "We're free!" Fern and Lily started to laugh, first cautiously, and then big eruptions of joy. Lily put her arm around her daughter and hugged her.

"Guess again." Fern spun around and found herself face to face with Henry Saagwalla. "Welcome to Casa Saagwalla," he said.

The House of Loss and Gain

"We're happy you're so eager to join us," Saagwalla gloated. Fern and Lily had made their great "escape" right smack into Henry Saagwalla's hideaway. It was a house built on a cliff overlooking the turquoise Indian Ocean. Every tunnel in the complex underground network intersected here at his hideout.

The building was barely visible above ground. It was built on a rocky plateau, and the far end abutted a cliff face that looked out to sea. The six-foot-long windows were perfectly camouflaged. The roof of the house was rock. The rest of it was so integrated into the landscape that you would never know a house existed there at all. It was an excellent hideout. No planes flying overhead could detect it. No boats at sea would spy it.

"Take them to the laboratory, Leslie," Saagwalla ordered.

Fern didn't like the sound of this at all. Aiming the Vapor-icer at his two captives, Leslie marched Fern and Lily down an endless hallway. Lily leaned on her daughter. Leslie carried the shell-shocked Silver Rose.

They passed through a gallery of photographs chronicling the triumphs of their captor. One photo highlighted a gaping hole in the earth in Romania. Dusty, weary men trudged down into the pit, carrying shovels and looking wretched. Henry Saagwalla stood in the foreground smiling, holding a giant lump of gold. In another photo, Henry posed in front of an Arctic vista as a geyser of black oil spewed out of the ground behind him. Polar bears streaked with black slime stood miserably in the background.

In yet another photo, thousands of tree stumps poked out of the ground, an entire tropical rain forest felled. Henry Saagwalla stood in the foreground, raising a thumbs-up. Behind him, jaguars wept as they searched for their missing homes. In a final portrait, a smiling Henry Saagwalla walked on a hillside covered with shriveled tea plants, their leaves dark with black fungus.

"What could make a man so evil?" asked Fern.

"Henry Saagwalla was once a beautiful boy and a scientific genius," Lily whispered, "but he was mistreated. He developed the most amazing tea plant in the world. Instead of being rewarded, he was punished for it, and was left terribly scarred by the very man whose respect he was trying to gain. Now he uses his genius to destroy the thing he used to love more than anything else . . . nature. I met him once in Darjeeling, India, when

I was trying to save the tea plantation in that photo. It was the only estate in the world that grew Saagwalla's own special, superior tea plant. It's all gone now."

"Do you know what he wants with us?" Fern asked.

"I don't," said Lily. "But it most certainly has to do with controlling and destroying nature."

"What are you two whispering about?" snapped Leslie. The two Verdants fell silent.

The corridor ended at a massive carved wooden door. Leslie ushered Fern and Lily through it into a large laboratory, all gleaming metallic surfaces and Bunsen burners and bottles filled with brightly colored liquids. In the middle of the room were two chairs. Rows of vials mounted on delicate wrought iron sconces hung on one wall. Each vial had a label on it. As Fern passed by she read them. *Hairless Bunny, Insane Happiness, Frog to Dog, Totally Humorless, Man to Pig, Spiderless Web, Plum to Onion, Man to Snake*, and the list went on and on. Fern thought it was a shame that Henry Saagwalla hadn't found a less evil way to use his brilliance.

Leslie put the Silver Rose on the counter. He pushed the Verdants toward the two chairs and strapped them both down. Fern scanned the room looking for something, anything that could help them escape. There were no windows, just gleaming, polished-metal walls. Beneath one wall full of cupboards was a counter with lots of test tubes and twin sinks. Leslie took a giant syringe out of a refrigerator.

"Henry Saagwalla is not going to get away with this," Fern said to Leslie, who guffawed and disappeared out the door.

"I am so sorry you're in this mess," sighed Lily. "And your poor father! He must be devastated; first me, then you."

"He has been pretty miserable."

"I feel bad that I spent so much time flying around the world rescuing failing flora instead of . . ." Lily's voice trailed off.

"And I'm sorry if I was an awful child."

"Don't be silly. You were never an awful child. I think one of the hardest things in the world is being thirteen years old. When I was thirteen, my mother and I didn't get along at all. To me, everything she did was wrong, and to her, everything I did was wrong. The gift brought us together. We had more in common than we realized. But you and I . . . well, one always thinks there's going to be more time." Lily was sad. A fall from a cliff, a trans-Pacific voyage, months in a cave in a coma, and a speeding train ride had left her exhausted and sentimental.

"Mom . . . I'm going to get us out of here."

"I don't want you doing anything dangerous!" Lily answered, weakly. Fern thought this seemed like an odd statement in light of where they were, but then a parent can't help being a parent.

"I have an idea. Please . . . try not to tell him anything. When he starts asking you questions, stall him for as long as you can, okay?" Fern was interrupted when Henry Saagwalla sauntered into the room wearing his lab coat. Leslie scrambled up behind him.

"Now then, let's continue where we left off before we were so rudely interrupted," Saagwalla said to Lily.

Fern looked past Saagwalla toward the counters that held

the gleaming sinks. Aside from the laboratory door, those two drains were the only other way in or out of this prison.

"You were saying?" Saagwalla continued. "You have a secret, and you're going to tell me all about it."

Fern looked at Lily. Lily looked at Fern. Lily cleared her throat.

"Secret?" Lily asked. "What secret?"

Saagwalla's look darkened. "Don't play games with me. I am renowned for my impatience. Tell me everything!"

Fern closed her eyes and focused as hard as she could.

"About what?" Lily looked blankly through heavy-lidded eyes.

"I've had enough!!" Saagwalla exploded. "No more stalling." He nodded toward Leslie. Leslie raised the syringe.

Fern concentrated. She blocked out Saagwalla, blocked out her mother, blocked everything out but the APB she was now desperately trying to get out beyond the thick metal walls. Saagwalla looked at Fern.

"What are *you* doing?" Fern's eyes remained closed. It was as if she was no longer in the same room as them, but somewhere far, far away.

"I said *what are you doing?*" Fern ignored him completely. Saagwalla was furious. There is nothing worse than a neglected villain.

"Please work this time—please work this time," Fern whispered under her breath.

"Have it your way." Saagwalla snapped his fingers, and Leslie stepped forth bearing the fully loaded syringe. "Truth serum. Not extremely imaginative, but it does the job. Now! Start talking. Explain your connection to the plant world!"

"I'm a botanist," stalled Lily. "I help plants." Saagwalla's face was getting red with anger.

Fern was focusing so hard, her head hurt. Leslie rolled up Lily's sleeve.

"Wait! I think it's coming to me . . . ," Lily bluffed to Leslie. Saagwalla was no fool. He knew these Verdants were toying with him, stalling for time. He nodded in Leslie's direction. Lily cried out as Leslie plunged the needle with the truth serum into her arm.

"No!!!!!!" Fern screamed, coming out of her trance. "Stop it!—Help us! Help us! Can't any of you hear me?"

"Any of who?" Saagwalla asked, puzzled. "Of course no one can hear you. This place is a vault." Then . . . the ground beneath the laboratory started to quietly vibrate. Saagwalla looked around, confused.

"Earthquake?" he muttered. "Hope it's a little one."

"You'll wish it was an earthquake!" Fern shouted at him.

Leslie pulled the needle out of Lily's arm, and her face took on a vague emptiness.

"Talk!" Saagwalla stared at her.

Lily's mouth opened. She seemed to be having some sort of internal struggle. The ground grumbled again.

"Mom! Noooo! Don't!" Fern cried out. But it was too late.

"When I was thirteen, my mother told me that I had the gift to communicate with plants; that it was my duty to save those in danger." Saagwalla's eyes were gleaming. "This gift was

passed down in our family from mother to daughter for generations. I don't know why or how. Only that it is."

Lily was horrified at what was coming out of her mouth, but
she couldn't stop it. Fern sighed, her shoulders sagged. Saagwalla looked as if he had just hit the jackpot.

"I speak with plants telepathically," continued Lily.

"Unbelievable!" Saagwalla's eyes opened wider. It was
better than he had hoped. Here in front of him was a way
to communicate with and control the entire plant world,
through two sources, no less! He was giddy with the prospect
of such power. So giddy that he wasn't paying attention to
the pushing and heaving and straining in the earth underneath him.

"How many people have this gift?" Saagwalla asked, looking
out of the corner of his eye at Fern.

"One," Lily replied very sadly. Saagwalla was confused. How
could that be, if the gift was passed from mother to daughter?
Why, there were two specimens right here in front of him!
When he opened his mouth to ask what Lily meant, a deafening explosion interrupted him.

Thousands of vines and creepers and plants blasted into the
room through the drains in the two shiny sinks. Thick, spaghetti-
like strands of undergrowth burst out everywhere, like emerald
Crazy String. They exploded with a whoosh. Saagwalla jumped
back, but the vines slithered across the floor with startling
speed, pouring out of the drains with such force that the sinks
themselves shot out of their counters. The vines raced toward
Saagwalla, who looked at them in horror.

"What?????" Saagwalla gasped. The vines groped at his ankles. Saagwalla climbed up onto a counter to escape them.

"Get away from me! Get away from me!" He shook his feet wildly as though performing a strange, convulsive dance. Saagwalla barely had time to react when a python-like creeper circled his waist, lifting his feet off the ground.

Leslie raised the Vapor-icer, but a vine strangled his wrist and sent the weapon skittering across the floor. Leslie cartwheeled toward the door, but his passage was blocked by a spiderweb of tightly woven creepers. When Leslie tried to launch away from them, he discovered his ankles were entwined in thick, ropy vines. They slithered and flopped all over the place, like live electric wires.

A creeper ripped the straps that tied Lily and Fern to their chairs.

"Run," it cried. "Get out of here . . . for the sake of all of us!"

Fern jumped to her feet, pulling her mother with her and grabbing the Silver Rose. The room exploded with greenery. Buds sprouted instantly into flowers. It was an indoor jungle, growing so quickly it sucked up all the space and air in the room. The two Verdants and the Silver Rose were practically pushed out the door by the expanding foliage.

Saagwalla and Leslie were about six feet off the ground, held in place by thick stalks and shoots, pressed tighter and tighter against the wall by the encroaching foliage, their backs against a row of vials full of Saagwalla's serums. Saagwalla struggled with the living restraints that held him pinned to the wall. He kicked and thrashed, but the vines were too strong. As the two

Verdants and the Silver Rose made their way to the door, the creepers shrank away from either side of it. Fern pushed the door open, and helped Lily and the Rose out to safety.

"Are you okay, Mom?"

Lily nodded her head. "I am." The Rose remained mute.

"Wait for me here, then; I'll be back in a minute." Fern quickly turned back toward the laboratory.

"Fern!" Lily called out.

With that, Fern disappeared into the room. There were so many vines and plants the place looked like a jungle. She edged past the two bound prisoners. Leslie's pasty arms and legs could barely move an inch. She quickly set about the task at hand. Fern plucked as many of Saagwalla's vials from the wall as she could carry. The scientist and his sidekick watched, restrained, unable to do a thing. Perhaps, she thought, just maybe, there was a potion to reverse the effects of Saagwalla's truth serum. Stuffing the vials into her pockets, she crept past the villains. She couldn't resist a final glance up at Saagwalla, trapped against the wall by the growth. She wished she hadn't. He gave her a look so venomous, so filled with hatred, her entire body went cold. Nearby, Fern noticed the Vapor-icer lying on the ground. She picked it up and fled, slamming and locking the laboratory door behind her.

Fern took Lily's arm and guided her down the hallway to the front door. The Silver Rose jounced in Lily's arms. Behind them they heard the swishing sounds of vines filling the room. In the foyer, they stopped to get their breath.

"Mom?" Fern looked at Lily. "Is it . . . is the gift really gone?"

"It's . . . gone." Lily sighed deeply. "I felt it leave." She looked very sad. "But I'm still a botanist, and I can still help plants. Most important of all, I still have you." Lily smiled. Even though the truth serum was still wearing off, Fern knew her mother was speaking from her heart.

As the two Verdants sat silently in the ebony foyer with the Silver Rose beside them, trying to absorb all that had happened, the front door of the house burst open. Olivier, Serge Cransac, and Anthony raced through it. Olivier saw his wife and daughter sitting on the floor, and an enormous smile spread across his face. He ran and hugged them.

"Lily! Fern! You're all right!" He was squeezing them so tightly they could hardly breathe. "I can barely believe it."

"Dad?" Fern was shocked to see Olivier Verdant halfway around the world in Sri Lanka, in the entrance to the Saagwalla hideout. "What are you doing here?"

"It's a very long story," Olivier said, then introduced them to Serge Cransac.

"Pleased to meet you." Fern nodded.

"*Mon dieu!* It is an honor to meet the granddaughter of Lisette Verdant." Serge bowed and took her hand. Over Serge's shoulder, Fern saw Anthony receding into the shadows. He was holding a bucket. She ran over to him.

"Anthony! What are you doing here?" Anthony shifted uncomfortably, not used to being the center of attention. "And how did you find us?"

"Your dad's plane was circling us with Marita Von Svenson

on board. He thought you were dead, but we told him you were alive."

"He volunteered to help us find you," Olivier added.

"They landed and picked me up. Marita Von Svenson had the coordinates for the cave." Anthony dropped his voice to a whisper. "I didn't say anything about the seaweed and the arrows."

Fern looked at him, surprised, grateful, and curious about what exactly he thought he knew. "Thank you."

"We found a creature . . . a Mant or maybe a Plan," said Olivier. "I'm not sure what he was, but he gave us your mother's note. The cave was wet and empty . . . except for . . . those . . ." Olivier pointed to the bucket in Anthony's hand. Anthony showed Fern its contents. The translucent, watery faces of Claude and Luella Hubris peered out from the bucket of water, not looking happy at all.

"They managed to gurgle out directions," said Anthony.

Just then Dr. Marita Von Svenson stepped inside the Saagwalla hideaway. "I want to see Henry Saagwalla!" she demanded.

"No, you don't!" Olivier then whispered to Fern, "She's hypnotized."

"No, I don't," Marita repeated obediently after him, and stepped back into the shadows.

"But I do," Serge Cransac said, ecstatic. "What a coup to capture such a renowned and evil man. He'll spend many, many years behind bars for these kidnappings and his crimes against the environment. I'm sure you'll get a reward for your bravery."

"He's a prisoner in his own laboratory." Fern handed the Vapor-icer to Serge Cransac. "You might need this. He's very clever."

Olivier stayed behind with Lily and the Silver Rose. Fern led Serge and Anthony to the laboratory. Serge trained the Vapor-icer on the laboratory door as Fern unlocked it. She flung it open, half expecting Saagwalla to pop out at her. But she found something entirely different. In the middle of a room full of rotted vines piled in heaps or clinging forlornly to the wall was an albino pig running in circles. It ran cowering into a corner.

"How did a pig get in here . . . and where's Henry Saagwalla?" Fern said, startled.

"It stinks in here," said Anthony.

"*Mon Dieu,*" said Serge, holding his nose. "Rotting flora!"

Fern couldn't believe the carnage. All of the vines that had come to their rescue had been killed. She felt horrible . . . worse than horrible. Then, something amid the tangle of dead plants caught her eye. Just beneath the wall where Saagwalla and Leslie had been held prisoner were pieces of broken glass. She knelt down. They were the remnants of Saagwalla's vials; the vials the scientist and Leslie had crushed as they were pressed up against the wall by the creepers.

The first vial read *Radical Rot.* Fern looked around sadly at all the shriveled plants, feeling terribly responsible. The second vial read *Man into Pig.* Leslie the albino pig squealed frantically from the corner. Fern picked up the third vial, which she knew would tell her what had happened to Henry Saagwalla. It read *Man into Snake*. As she finished reading the label, her thoughts were interrupted by a sound . . . a hissing sound. Fern stood up and looked around. Across the room, where the sinks had once been, a large brown cobra was disappearing down one of the exposed drains in the counter. By the time Serge understood what was happening and fired the Vapor-icer into the darkness of the drain, the snake was nowhere to be seen.

Outside the Saagwalla hideout, Albert Wedgie stood stiffly waiting for the others. He squinted at something strange in the distance. A patch of brown grass shriveled away from a swiftly slithering giant cobra. The cobra moved quickly over the ground, under a blanket of shadow created by a sky full of black bats. It was long gone by the time Fern and the others raced outside.

The Next to Last Bit

"I don't understand this. Why? Why on earth would Henry Saagwalla want to kidnap you, Lily?" Olivier asked.

"I really don't know why," Lily fibbed.

"It doesn't make any sense!"

"It's because she talks to plants," interrupted Fern, "just like every botanist speaks to plants."

"Excuse me," Claude Hubris piped up from his bucket. "If you'll just go into that laboratory, I'm sure you'll find some Vaporicer restorative serum that might be of help to Luella and me. We'd be grateful if you'd return us to our former selves." Fern looked at the bucket, feeling just a little bit sorry for the Hubrises.

"There was no such vial in the room," said Fern. Claude and Luella both looked as dismal as villains turned trees turned puddles could look.

"Your wife really can talk to plants," gurgled Luella angrily. Olivier sighed.

"All botanists talk to plants," Olivier answered, getting really tired of explaining this over and over. Anthony looked at Fern curiously, knowing full well there was more to it than that.

There was a great deal of explaining to do on everyone's part. So many secrets had been hidden over the years. Fern and Lily were both very surprised to hear about the Resistance, and about Grandmamma Lisette's involvement in it. They were secretly pleased that Olivier had taken to international intrigue like a duck to water. He was like a kid with a new train when he told them about things like super-powered binoculars and GPS tracking devices. Olivier telephoned Grandmamma Lisette, who was overjoyed to learn that her son had successfully retrieved the rest of the family.

Serge Cransac suggested he airlift everyone back to the beach. When they tried to transport Leslie the albino pig, he squealed and fought so much, they left him behind, roaming outside the Saagwalla hideout with lots of food. Albert Wedgie lumbered onto the plane, making it a tight squeeze since he could no longer sit like a person, but had to lie like a log. They contemplated tying him to a pontoon but determined it was too risky. Dr. Marita Von Svenson sat crammed uncomfortably beside him, with a branch poking into her ribs, but she'd been ordered not to complain, and so she didn't.

Francesca brought the Silver Petal and the orphans to shore in the dinghy. The children were delighted to see Anthony and Fern, but not so delighted to see the adults with them. They built a great roaring fire on the beach. Everyone sat around it, including the bucket of Hubrises. It seemed rude to just let them dry up and disappear. Kai was very taken with them. He'd always wanted pets. He took it upon himself to replenish their water when it began to evaporate. When he accidentally put some sea water in the bucket, both Hubrises fell into coughing fits.

Although Lily was happy to be with her family again, there was a strange sadness about her. Olivier could never have guessed the cause, but Fern was worried.

"I'm fine, really!" Lily insisted weakly, holding her husband's hand. Fern knew the sadness went deep. It was the sadness of someone who realizes they're no longer who they once were.

There was a big, sobbing, rust-inducing scene as the Petal was reunited with the Silver Rose. Of course, no one was witness to that emotional reunion but Fern.

Everyone was exhausted as they sat around the fire at dusk. Fern was grateful to Anthony, Francesca, and the rest of the orphans. Without them she could never have found her mother. But all the kids were painfully aware that they had exposed themselves as refugee orphans. They were miserable and huddled off to one side of the fire. What would become of them?

On the other side of the fire, Fern sat by her mother and father and Serge.

"Those poor children are all alone." Lily was a mother, and couldn't help but be concerned. "They need to be taken care of."

"It's far too dangerous a world to have children roaming

about unguided," added Olivier. There was no arguing with the adults, who were all responsible people. They agreed it was their duty to report the children's whereabouts to the authorities, so good foster homes could be found and the children could go to school and the dentist.

"But the adults who cared for them before treated them terribly!" said Fern.

Olivier had explained to Lily all about NITPIC and the evil Dr. Von Svenson. He had grown tired of Von Svenson's chatter. "Find the good in yourself . . . there's got to be some goodness somewhere inside of you," he'd ordered. Suddenly Marita didn't look particularly threatening as she sat by the fire roasting some marshmallows Lulu had brought to shore. Olivier turned his attention back to the orphans.

"It would be reckless to leave a boatload of young orphans floating around on the Indian Ocean," Olivier said.

"Your father is right. What if something happened to them because they were without adult supervision?" Lily added.

"Perhaps the Resistance could help find a good orphanage for them?" Serge added. None of the adults were thrilled about having to take this course of action, but what was the alternative?

Anthony overheard the entire conversation.

"Do you think they'll just let us go off on our own?" Francesca whispered to her brother.

"No, they're adults, and they always think they know best."

"Perhaps we should sail away in the middle of the night," rasped Jane, eager for further adventure.

"It wouldn't matter," Anthony said. "They know our boat, our names, everything . . . they'd find us quickly." Lulu glumly served up coconut fritters, while Tim wondered if there was somewhere they could go that didn't exist on a map.

"I told you so." Kai was fighting back tears. "Now what's going to happen to us?" Francesca put her arm around him. They were all worried.

It had been quite a long day. Gradually, most everyone dozed off around the campfire. Everyone, that is, except Fern, who dug out the vials she'd hidden in her pockets. She read the labels, searching for one in particular that she had noticed back in Saagwalla's laboratory. She smiled as she separated it from the others, stuffing the rest in her backpack.

Farther down the beach Fern saw that Anthony and Francesca were awake. They sat in the moonlight staring sadly out to sea. She wandered down the sand toward them.

"This is our thanks for helping you?" Anthony snapped angrily.

"What makes them think we are better off with adults?" Francesca asked.

"I've been thinking," said Fern. "Why don't you take over Henry Saagwalla's secret hideout? It's quite big, it's hidden, and with a little landscaping it could be beautiful. He won't be returning. It's not a secret hideout for him anymore."

"But your parents?" Anthony said. "They're going to report us."

"No, I don't think they will." Fern held out her hand. In her palm was one of the vials from Saagwalla's laboratory. Anthony read the label *Forgetting Serum* and smiled. It was the first time Fern had seen him really smile.

The next morning Lulu and Jane made all the adults a delicious breakfast of oatmeal cakes with coconut butter. They brought a teapot and cups from the *Porpoise*. Fern served up a big steaming pot of tea.

"It's beautiful Ceylon tea from right here on this island," Fern said. Each of the adults took a sip and agreed it was indeed wonderful. Fern watered Albert Wedgie with a little of the serum.

"What were we talking about?" Lily looked puzzled.

"Serge, Mom, Dad . . . ," Fern said, ". . . and you too, Albert Wedgie. As soon as we leave this island, you will forget you ever met the orphans. As far as you're concerned, they do not exist." Then Fern turned to her mother. She took a big breath. This next command was hard for Fern to make.

"Mom." Fern had thought about this all night. Lily's heartbroken expression helped make up Fern's mind. She whispered in her mother's ear, "You will forget you ever had the gift of talking to plants." Lily's face instantly softened and lost its sadness, assuming the contented expression it once had.

"What a ridiculous man . . . kidnapping a botanist!" Lily said.

Olivier put his hand on his wife's. "Indeed!"

259

The Very Last Bit

When it was time to return home, it was decided that Serge Cransac would fly the Verdant family, the Silver Rose, and Albert Wedgie back to Nedlaw.

"I wouldn't have my family together, if it weren't for all of you," Fern said to the orphans.

Francesca hugged Fern tightly. "I always wanted a sister, and now I feel like I have one."

Fern hugged each of the orphans, except Anthony, who was just not a hugger, and Kai, who had disappeared somewhere. As the adults boarded the plane, Anthony approached Fern. "Thank you for helping us to stay free." He stared at her, in a way that made her uncomfortable. Fern blushed. "If you ever need our help in the future," he added, "you know where we are."

The orphans stood on the shoreline and watched as everyone got on board the plane. Kai came running down the beach. He tugged on Fern's sleeve.

"And thank you for finding us a home." From behind his back, Kai presented a bouquet of beautiful orchids. Fern gasped.

"I know, they're pretty, aren't they?" Kai grinned. Fern was horrified—until she remembered that cutting the bloom had nothing to do with the life of the plant. There was so much to get used to in this new world she'd been exposed to. She kissed Kai on the cheek.

Fern waved from the plane as it took off. The adults looked out the aircraft windows and tried to figure out who it was they were waving goodbye to.

The orphans boarded the *Porpoise* and sailed to Saagwalla's hideaway. They decided that they would take Dr. Marita Von Svenson with them. She was still hypnotized and quite easy to control. Besides, they could use an adult to run errands for them. Francesca and Anthony particularly enjoyed ordering her about. Fern told the adults they'd better forget about Marita Von Svenson as well. She didn't want any nosey authorities snooping after the orphans. The bucket of Hubrises was taken along and put in a pond. It became Kai's chore to make sure there was enough water in the pond so the couple didn't dry up and disappear. He also ended up in charge of feeding Leslie the pig.

Back in Nedlaw, Albert Wedgie was admitted to a botanical research facility, where after many months of study, care, and nurturing, he was returned to his former human state. Albert showed the kind of mettle he was made of by rejoining Trees Pleese and becoming even more devoted to spreading the word of greater greenery throughout the world. He became their most successful fund-raiser. If anyone knew how tough it was to be a tree, it was Albert.

Grandmamma Lisette was overjoyed to see her family together and stayed with them for a whole month until everyone seemed to be back to normal. Serge Cransac flew Grandmamma home to Paris. Serge, Fern noted, seemed quite fond of Grandmamma.

Olivier returned to his ferns. Lily returned to botany, though without so much travel. Lily seemed more "normal" than before; more like a regular mother. She even started straightening her hair. It was as if she had lost some wild part of herself. Fern missed the old Lily.

Fern kept the Silver Rose on a table by her bedside. The Trumpet Flower was initially jealous, but it eventually took pride in sharing space with what had become a legendary flower. The Rose had been greatly saddened by the loss of its friendship with Lily Verdant, but neither the Rose nor Fern could imagine Lily spending the rest of her life in such sorrow. It was better that she never knew she'd had the gift, instead of mourning its loss forever. Lily was able to graft the Petal to the Rose. She was, after all, still an excellent botanist. The Silver Rose was the only friend Fern could talk to that fully understood everything that had occurred. It had spent so much time with Lily that it had acquired tremendous wisdom about her relationship with the plant world. It was comforting for Fern to have the Silver Rose as a friend.

Fern had transported Saagwalla's vials of serum home with her. There were about a dozen of them. She knew that someday they might come in handy. One afternoon, not long after the family's return to Nedlaw, Fern consulted with the Silver Rose. She wanted to find a perfect hiding place for the vials. They agreed that a deep hollow in an old Oak on the Verdant property would be perfect. "Forget that big-mouth Willow," the Rose had warned. Fern asked the Oak to guard the vials, and the Oak graciously accepted the assignment. Fern sat on her bed, wrapping each vial in thick gauze. She was placing them carefully in a shoebox when she heard a strange sound, a loud, sorrowful weeping, mournful and sad. Fern looked around the room. It took her a moment to realize the voice was coming from somewhere inside her head.

"Help me!" its plaintive cry repeated over and over. "Help me!" It was such a forlorn sound, heartbreaking to hear.

"Fern Verdant! I am the last one!" Fern went to her window and looked into the distance. She gazed out past the slim sliver of gray sea, out to the whole wide world beyond it, and listened as a beautiful teal Tulip blooming in a Tunisian garden cried out for help.

About the Author

Diana Leszczynski has wanted to write books for as long as she can remember. But instead she did a bunch of different jobs, including reporting, researching, developing films, and teaching yoga. She traveled around the world and saw many amazing things. Finally she decided it was time to write. *Fern Verdant & the Silver Rose* is her first novel, and she is busily at work on her next.

She was born in England, raised in Canada, and now lives in California with her husband and a cat named Mouse.